Lo Simpson
Starts a
Revolution

Lo Simpson
Starts a
Revolution

Melanie Florence

ORCA BOOK PUBLISHERS

Published in Canada and the United States in 2024 by Orca Book Publishers.
orcabook.com

Library and Archives Canada Cataloguing in Publication
Title: Lo Simpson starts a revolution / Melanie Florence.
Names: Florence, Melanie, author.
Identifiers: Canadiana (print) 20230485790 | Canadiana (ebook) 20230485804 |
ISBN 9781459838505 (softcover) | ISBN 9781459838512 (PDF) |
ISBN 9781459838529 (EPUB)
Subjects: LCGFT: Novels.
Classification: LCC PS8611.L668 L62 2024 | DDC jC813/.6—dc23

Library of Congress Control Number: 2023942271

Summary: In this middle-grade novel, Lo's best friend, Jazz,
is leaving her behind for the popular crowd, makeup and boys. But when
Lo finds new friends who share her love of comics and *Doctor Who*, she also
discovers her voice—and the confidence to speak up for what's right.

Orca Book Publishers is committed to reducing the consumption
of nonrenewable resources in the production of our books. We make
every effort to use materials that support a sustainable future.

Orca Book Publishers gratefully acknowledges the support for its publishing
programs provided by the following agencies: the Government of Canada,
the Canada Council for the Arts and the Province of British Columbia
through the BC Arts Council and the Book Publishing Tax Credit.

Cover design by Troy Cunningham
Cover image by Mike Deas
Edited by Sarah Howden
Author photo by Ian Crysler

Printed and bound in Canada.

27 26 25 24 • 1 2 3 4

For all my fellow Whovians.
And for anyone who, like me, fought growing up.
Trust me—you're going to be just fine.

ONE

Lo was wearing her brand-new *Doctor Who* cosplay for the very first time when her best friend, Jazz, announced that they should go shopping for bras together.

It was one of those spring days that smelled like summer in the backyard. Like coconut-scented sunscreen, strawberry lemonade and freshly mown grass.

And underneath all that, Lo thought she could smell a hint of the lemon juice that Jazz religiously drizzled in her hair because she absolutely insisted that it gave her natural highlights.

Lo thought it smelled like sunshine, if sunshine had a scent. It smelled like every single summer day that Lo had spent giggling and plotting with Jazz in her backyard since the second grade.

The sun was beating down relentlessly on her neck as she let herself through the gate and into Jazz's backyard. And there she was. Her best friend in the world. Lying in the sun, crisping like a piece of bacon in a fire-engine-red bikini that Lo wouldn't be caught dead in. The last time *she* sunbathed, Lo had covered up in an old one-piece, faded gray from being washed and hung to dry in the sun so many times.

Lo cleared her throat until Jazz looked up.

"Well?" she asked, extending her arms and spinning around. She stopped and pulled out her sonic screwdriver and pointed it at Jazz dramatically, holding her pose until she got a response.

"Well what?" Jazz asked, adjusting her bikini bottom and reaching for the sunscreen.

Not *that* kind of response.

"What do you think?" Lo asked. Was Jazz serious? Lo had worked her butt off on her cosplay. She had nearly cried with joy when they announced that the new Doctor was going to be a woman, and she'd started working on her cosplay the second she saw the amazing outfit the new Doctor would be wearing on the show. She had ordered the suspenders in the exact color of mustard yellow that the Thirteenth Doctor wore. She had gone to every single shoe store in the city to find the right boots. She had spent every last dollar she'd earned babysitting on a custom-made jacket that was perfect right down to the rainbow piping that you couldn't even see from the outside but was absolutely vital to have if you were going to be the Doctor.

Jazz shrugged. "Your hair is the wrong color."

Lo touched the ends of her dark hair. She had talked her mom into letting her get Thirteen's awesomely cool bob, but she wasn't about to bleach it blond, and she couldn't afford a decent wig. Not yet anyway. But other than her hair, her outfit was absolutely perfect!

"That's it?" Lo asked.

"Okay, the rest of it is good," Jazz said with a complete lack of enthusiasm.

"Good?"

"It's good, Lo. Jeez. I'm just not really into cosplay."

Was she serious? Since when? Last year Jazz had spent months perfecting every tiny detail of her Weeping Angels cosplay and made Lo watch every episode of *Doctor Who* featuring the creepy angel statues repeatedly so she could practice posing like them.

"Jazz, I worked hard on this. And I'll have a wig by the time we go to FanCon, so it'll be perfect."

"Whatever. It's great. Sorry. I've just had other stuff going on. You know?" Jazz said, rubbing sunscreen into her already brown legs and avoiding Lo's eyes. "Anyway. How do you expect to get a tan dressed like that?"

Lo rolled her eyes and took her jacket off, hanging it carefully over the back of a chair. She took off her boots and socks and sat down beside Jazz on a towel scratchy-stiff from hanging out on the laundry line in the sunshine.

"Happy now?" she asked, pouring herself some lemonade and smacking her lips at the tangy sweetness. Jazz shrugged and pulled her curly hair into a messy knot on the top of her head and secured it with a scrunchie printed with bright-blue butterflies.

Lo looked around the yard, sucking lazily on an ice cube, and watched a fat green caterpillar inching its way across a long blade of grass.

I'd rather be a caterpillar than a butterfly, she thought idly, glancing over at Jazz, who had lost interest in their conversation and was watching some beauty vlogger on her iPad. Jazz studied makeup tutorials and fashion advice single-mindedly, the way Lo pored through library books.

Jazz used to read library books too, Lo thought. And she used to love *Doctor Who* as much as Lo did.

Jazz looked up at her through pink, heart-shaped sunglasses that slipped down her nose when she tilted her head.

"We should go bra shopping," she said.

TWO

Lo choked on her ice cube until Jazz smacked her on the back.

"Why would we want to go bra shopping?" Lo sputtered.

"Because we're, like, the only two girls in our grade who don't wear a bra."

Lo seriously doubted that.

The caterpillar had disappeared from its blade of grass. Obviously it was as horrified as Lo was by the direction this conversation had taken.

Lo hoped the caterpillar would form a chrysalis soon. She and Jazz put one in a jar every single year and watched it change inside the little cocoon it built around itself, metamorphosing until it hatched into an orange-and-black monarch. She loved that word. *Metamorphosing*. Changing into something new. Which Lo was all for, as long as that change didn't involve wearing some medieval torture device wrapped around her rib cage!

"But we don't need bras," she said firmly. She was willing to bet the Doctor never had to deal with such *embarrassing* things. Her face burned.

"Yes, we do," Jazz insisted.

Jazz was always insisting on things, and Lo almost always went along with whatever she said because it was easier than arguing.

But a bra?

Lo was sure it would feel exactly like wearing a straitjacket. Like the Eleventh Doctor in "Day of the Moon." If he were a girl. Like Thirteen.

"We're not little kids anymore, Lo," Jazz told her.

But that was exactly what Lo felt like. Twelve was too young for the things Jazz seemed to like now. Makeup and boys and expensive jeans and high heels and bras! Lo's idea of fashion was a Spider-Man T-shirt and cut-off jean shorts. Or her new Thirteenth Doctor cosplay.

She liked Spider-Man and *Doctor Who*. She liked comic books and superheroes and her perfectly scuffed red Converse sneakers. She still slept with a stuffed animal! And if she was being really and truly honest, Lo secretly still sort of believed that alternate dimensions existed. She even kind of believed in magic. Just not the kind of magic that made girls giggle like idiots at boys like Jason Lieberman, who was so annoying she wanted to scream.

"We're only twelve," Lo reminded her.

"We're nearly thirteen! Just come to the mall with me, Lo. Jeez. It's no big deal."

Lo stared at her. Jazz had been her best friend since she had pushed Bobby Zucker into the mud in second grade for telling Lo she looked like a horse. But sometimes Lo felt like she barely knew her anymore.

"Fine," she said, sighing. "But I'm not getting changed."

She'd come back outside and find a chrysalis later when she was by herself.

THREE

Lo wasn't sure she was ready to tell her mom she was going shopping for a bra. Her mom was actually pretty cool as far as moms went, but how cool could *any* mom really be? Her mom listened to the oldies station and sang along at the top of her lungs when one of her favorite David Bowie songs came on. And no one (except possibly David Bowie himself) looked cool screaming "CH-CH-CHANGES!" out the car window. But she was really big on talking through stuff, and Lo wasn't sure she was ready yet to talk about bras—and, by extension, breasts—with her mom. Maybe she'd keep this particular shopping trip to herself.

She had used all her babysitting money on her cosplay, so this called for birthday money.

In other words, it called for raiding the piggy bank she had painstakingly painted to look like Spider-Man and who she affectionately called Spider-Pig. She picked up the little ceramic pig and started dejectedly fishing out the cash she had been saving for a wig to complete her cosplay. She couldn't believe she was wasting her wig money on a bra!

"God, Lo. Aren't you ready yet?" Jazz threw herself down on the bed dramatically.

Lo glanced at her, then did a double take. "What did you do to your face?"

Jazz raised an eyebrow. "It's just a little makeup," she said, frowning.

Lo should have stopped as soon as she saw Jazz's frown, but it was just so funny! Because it was like saying that her aunt Megan, who currently looked like she had swallowed a basketball, was "just a little pregnant."

"It looks like a paint store exploded all over your face." Lo laughed, expecting Jazz to laugh with her and wash the rainbow of colors off. Jazz wasn't just frowning anymore, though. She looked absolutely disgusted. But she shrugged and tossed her curls as if she couldn't be bothered to get angry.

"You're such a child," she sniffed. "If you're coming, let's go." She studied Lo for a second. "Don't you want to get changed?"

Lo glanced down at her outfit. "I said I wasn't going to," she said.

"I thought you were kidding. What if we run into someone?"

"Like who?" Lo wondered who they could possibly run into who would (a) be surprised by her outfit or (b) care what she was wearing.

"Like...I don't know." Jazz looked at herself in the mirror and twisted a curl around her finger. "Like Jason Lieberman."

Ugh. Why did everyone—including Jason Lieberman himself—think he was so great?

"Jason Lieberman is stuck-up," Lo told her.

"No he's not! Everyone at school except you thinks he's nice."

"Yeah, well…he doesn't fool me," Lo muttered.

"Whatever. You look like a little kid in that outfit."

Jazz turned and stalked out of the room. Lo looked down at herself, then at Jazz's retreating back. Next to Jazz, she *did* look like a kid. Next to Jazz, Lo *felt* like a kid. But I mean, come on! she said to herself. They weren't even thirteen yet!

Lo sighed and grabbed a pen. "I'll be there in a second," she called to Jazz. She needed to write something down before she chased after her friend.

Just like she always did.

So before she ran after Jazz and went to the mall to try on bras—which she *really* didn't want to spend her Saturday doing—Lo grabbed a binder she had been decorating with stickers and quotes for years and turned to a new blank page.

Dear Doctor, she wrote.

FOUR

Lo could still remember the very first time she laid eyes on the Doctor. She was ten years old and home sick with a raging case of mono—NOT kissing-related, she told everyone repeatedly when they teased her. She was lying on the couch, wrapped in a fleece blanket like a cozy-soft burrito, alternating between being bored out of her mind and sleeping several hours at a time. She was awake and channel surfing, figuring she had about forty-five minutes before she needed another nap, when she landed on a channel showing old episodes of British shows and saw the big blue box for the very first time in her life. The TARDIS. The TARDIS was hurtling through space—a phone box in space!—and landed in Central London, and out stepped the man who would change Lo's entire life.

The Tenth Doctor.

The absolute coolest person Lo had ever seen.

He was dressed in a bright-blue suit and red Converse sneakers that Lo immediately knew she had to own herself.

He was funny and clever and brave and adventurous and loyal. Everything Lo wasn't. And after that one episode, Lo knew she wanted to be just like him.

Dear Doctor,
I think I'm losing my best friend.
Sincerely,
Lo

FIVE

The mall was packed with kids killing time, shopping for things they didn't really need and eating things their parents would never approve of. Mothers were pushing strollers around aimlessly, trying to keep their babies calm while zombie-like shoppers rushed from store to store in search of sales.

Jazz clearly was still pissed off, striding a full step ahead of Lo and never once turning to check that she was keeping up. She stopped suddenly in front of Victoria's Secret, its window full of blown-up photos of supermodels in thongs and push-up bras. Every imaginable color of lace and silk was on display, along with something called a water bra that promised to add two full cup sizes.

Lo felt her cheeks burn. There was *no way in hell* she was setting foot in there. She caught Jazz studying her and rolling her eyes.

"No way, Jazz," she warned. Which was really not like her, when she stopped and thought about it. Maybe the

Thirteenth Doctor's cosplay was making her brave.

"Fine!" Jazz said, "God, Lo. Did you have to wear that? Everyone is staring at you!"

She was right. And normally Lo hated being the center of attention. But she wasn't Lo today. She was the Doctor. And that was so much cooler than being just plain old, boring Lo Simpson. She whipped her sonic screwdriver out of her jacket pocket and pointed it at a kid in a stroller who grinned and waved a sippy cup back at her.

"Will you put that thing away! God, you're so embarrassing!" Jazz hissed.

Lo tucked it back into her pocket and let Jazz lead her toward the other side of the mall, where the doorway to Justify beckoned.

Lo felt herself relax instantly. She had been in here with her mother a million times for jeans and T-shirts. And she and Jazz had bought matching sloth onesies here the year before, which they had gleefully worn as pajamas or regular outfits, depending on their moods. Jazz led the way to the back corner where pj's, underwear and bras hung on the walls.

It's fine, Lo told herself, taking a deep breath. She looked down at her Thirteenth Doctor shirt with its bright rainbow stripes and willed it to send her strength. *It's just any other day. Just another trip to the mall. You're definitely not here shopping for bras. Nope. Not at all.*

But that's exactly what she was doing.

Or at least Jazz was doing it. With almost single-minded determination.

Lo watched Jazz take down hanger after hanger, fingering lace in shades of pink and blue without caring who might be watching.

"What do you think of this one?" she asked Lo, holding a heavily padded bra up in front of her.

Lo blushed, looking around quickly to see if anyone really *was* watching. Luckily, no one had even noticed them in the corner of the busy store.

Jazz rolled her eyes for what seemed like the seventy-third time since leaving the house.

"Ummm. It's nice, I guess?"

"Well, let's try some stuff on."

Jazz had at least a dozen bras in different colors and materials. Lo reached up and grabbed a gray sports bra that practically covered more of her than her bathing suit did.

"I'll try this one," she said, balling it up so no one would see. She caught Jazz rolling her eyes again. I hope they get stuck that way, Lo thought, sticking out her tongue behind Jazz's back.

SIX

Jazz rolling her eyes at her was nothing new to Lo. She remembered the first time like it had happened yesterday.

It was right after Lo had discovered *Doctor Who* and was eager to get her best friend to watch it with her and fall in love with the show like she had.

"I saw the coolest episode last night—you'd love this one, I swear." Lo was so excited, she was literally bouncing in her seat.

"What's it about again?" Jazz asked, taking a delicate bite of a cracker smeared with sunflower butter.

Lo took a quick drink from her water bottle and then dove right in.

"So it's about a Time Lord—the Doctor—and he travels through time and space in a blue phone box called the TARDIS. It's amazing! He gets to go to all these cool places, and sometimes he fights alien races, and he has friends called Companions who travel with him because he's the last of his kind. It's just so cool, Jazz!"

Lo stuffed a cookie into her mouth and nearly swallowed it whole in her excitement. She choked—of course—and Jazz had to pound her on the back and hand her the bottle of water, which Lo chugged gratefully. She saw Bobby Zucker laughing at her and stuck her tongue out to show him she didn't care what he thought.

"You okay? So what was this episode about?" Jazz asked.

"Thanks! So anyway. The cutest little squishy, puffy guys were in this one, Jazz. I thought they were the bad guys, but they weren't! And omigosh, Jazz! They're called Adipose, and they're made from people's fat!" she finished breathlessly. She reached for her last two cookies, fully intending to share one with Jazz, whose parents didn't pack treats in her lunch. But at the mention of fat, Jazz's nose crinkled up.

"That's disgusting!" she said, taking a bite of her apple slice.

"No! They're actually really cute! I swear. You should come over after school. I recorded it for you."

"I don't know why you watch that show," Jazz said, rolling her eyes in a way that Lo would come to recognize over the years as Jazz's signature move that could mean anything from boredom to disgust and always shut down any further discussion. And the funny thing was, Jazz ended up finally watching and loving *Doctor Who* as much as Lo did. But in that moment, Lo had felt like this show—this character—that meant everything to her was dumb. All because Jazz had rolled her eyes.

SEVEN

They shared a changeroom, just like they had for years. Lo and Jazz had been changing in front of each other since they were seven, so it really shouldn't have been a big deal. But the way Jazz threw her clothes off so enthusiastically while Lo twisted herself into a pretzel to cover as much of herself as humanly possible was kind of awkward. She hadn't been uncomfortable like this with Jazz until recently, Lo realized.

Everything had changed this year.

Lo managed to get out of her T-shirt and struggle into the sports bra without standing stark naked in the middle of the cramped changeroom. Or worse, being shoved out through the curtain and into the middle of the busy store so everyone would see her standing there in a bra and laugh. Which she was sure was about to happen every time Jazz turned suddenly to look in the mirror from another weird position. But Jazz seemed pretty comfortable half-naked, checking out each bra she tried on from every possible angle.

If Lo was going to wear a bra—and she had no intention of actually wearing one—the sports bra wasn't completely awful. It flattened out any curve that happened to be popping up.

"What do you think?" Jazz asked, throwing her chest out and staring at herself in the mirror. She had developed more than Lo had realized.

"It's nice?" she said, trying not to look too closely at her friend's chest.

"Does it make my boobs look bigger?"

"What? I don't know!" Lo said, her face burning. "Jeez, Jazz!"

"Well, look!" Jazz insisted.

Lo peeked as quickly as she possibly could before looking away again. "Ummm…yes?"

"And isn't the lace pretty? I love it so much!" Jazz squealed.

Lo couldn't even fathom a response to that one. She loved it? A bra? Lo wished desperately for this to be over. The only thing she wanted in the entire world right now was to go get frozen yogurt with as many toppings as she could pile onto it and browse through the clearance racks at Hot Stuff, the store across the mall that carried things from every conceivable fandom, including those weird stuffed animals with what looked like real human teeth. They were so ugly they gave Lo the shivers.

"I'm getting it," Jazz announced, pulling it off and adding it to the growing pile of lingerie she intended to buy. She stood half-naked, not caring at all if Lo saw her, separated from the entire mall by only a flimsy blue curtain on a couple of shower rings, and pulled her shirt back over her head.

She wrenched the curtain open and screamed. Lo leaped in front of her, ready to defend her friend from danger if necessary. But the only threat she could see were the "It Girls"—the most popular girls in their grade.

"Jazzi!" the lead It Girl shrieked at a pitch so high Lo half-expected the store windows to shatter.

Jazzi? Since when did anyone call her Jazzi? And so clearly with an *i*. Probably dotted with a little heart too. Now the It Girls and Jazz were all screaming and jumping up and down together.

No one said hi to Lo.

No one even seemed to notice she was there.

"What are you *doing* here?" Abbi—also with an *i* and *definitely* dotted with a heart—asked *way, way* too loudly.

"Buying bras!" Jazz yelled back.

"Oh my god! I have that one!" Abbi cried out, pulling her sleeve off her shoulder to show the strap.

"Me too!" the others screamed.

There were far too many bra straps showing for Lo's taste. And far too many girls screaming about it loud enough for everyone on this side of the mall to hear.

"Do you want to come with us for froyo?" Abbi asked, linking her arm with Jazz's.

"Oh my god! Yes! Just let me pay for these."

Her gaze landed on Lo.

Yep. I'm still here. Lo cocked an eyebrow.

"Oh...ummm..." Jazz glanced between Lo and Abbi. "I'm actually here with Lo."

"Who?" Abbi asked, looking right past Lo for someone cooler or less *Doctor Who*-ish.

"Me," Lo said, her face burning. They'd been in the same class for years, and Abbi didn't know who she was. She turned to Jazz. "It's fine," Lo told her. "You go ahead."

"Really? I mean…do you *want* to come?" Jazz asked, shifting from one foot to the other and clearly hoping she'd say no.

"I don't really feel like frozen yogurt," Lo lied. She absolutely refused to call it *froyo*. "Seriously. Just go ahead."

"Are you sure?" Jazz was already edging away from her. Away from Lo and toward Abbi with an *i* and the other It Girls and their lacy bra straps.

"Yeah. Of course. You guys have fun." She flapped an arm, waving at them like…well, like the awkward kid she was.

"K! Talk later!"

The It Girls pulled Jazz—sorry, *Jazzi*—away before the words were even out of Lo's mouth. Not one of them had even acknowledged her. No one looked back toward her at all. Except Abbi. Abbi stared at Lo and then stage-whispered to Jazz so loudly the entire store turned to look.

"What is she wearing?"

Lo felt her face burning, but she thought of Thirteen and held her head up. "I'm the Doctor," she told Abbi.

Abbi cocked her head to the side. "Doctor who?"

"Exactly!" Lo laughed and looked at Jazz, expecting her to join in. But Jazz was looking down, jaw clenched, refusing to meet her eyes. Lo's laughter died on her lips.

"I don't get it," Abbi said, tossing her hair and leading Jazz away toward the cashiers and the other It Girls. "She's so weird! She doesn't even look like a doctor. She doesn't even have, like, a stethoscope or anything."

She waited for Jazz to defend her—to tell her new friends that she was wearing the official Thirteenth Doctor cosplay— but Jazz didn't say a word. She just shrugged and admired the lip gloss one of the other girls held out. Lo's eyes prickled. Nope. She would not let a bunch of girls who wouldn't know the difference between a Dalek and the TARDIS if one landed on them make her cry. She stuffed the sports bra under a pile of T-shirts and headed directly to Hot Stuff, the shrieks and giggles of the four It Girls ringing in her ears.

Dear Doctor,

The It Girls laughed at me, and my best friend didn't say a word to them. You know how the Doctor always has a Companion to count on? Someone they'd die for and who would always have their back in return? That's Jazz. Or it used to be. She was always there, always had my back, no matter what. But today, for the first time, my Amy Pond laughed along with the people making fun of me.

And it sucked.

Your friend always,

Lo

EIGHT

The first time Lo had written to the Doctor—David Tennant, or Ten in that case—she'd just wanted to tell him how much she loved the show and how she wanted to be just like him. She tracked down a studio address online, took an envelope and stamp from the kitchen drawer and mailed the letter with shaking hands.

Every day for weeks she ran home after school and checked the mailbox, knowing the Doctor would recognize a kindred spirit and respond.

He never did.

And that was okay. She knew David Tennant was busy doing whatever it was he was doing now that someone else was playing the Doctor. And maybe he hadn't even gotten her letter. To be honest, she wasn't even really writing to *him*. The actor. She was writing to the Doctor. That's who she felt a connection with. So she kept writing the Doctor letters, which she folded and kept in a box on the top shelf of her closet. Like a journal. Because if anyone could help her figure out her crazy life, it was the Doctor.

NINE

"What did you get up to today?" Lo's mom asked, slicing vegetables for a salad. She was really big on having salad with dinner. "Always have something green on your plate" was her motto. Lo, thinking she was clever, had once asked her mom how that worked for breakfast and suddenly started getting kiwi and honeydew slices with her cereal.

"I went to the mall," Lo said.

"With Jazz?"

"Yeah."

"Were you shopping? Or…?" her mom asked.

"Just walking around. Hanging out. Whatever." Lo shrugged.

"Ah. Well. Let me know next time you go, and I'll give you some money. You could use some new school clothes." Her mom turned back to her chopping.

"I like my clothes," Lo grumbled.

"Okay. That's fine. It's up to you," her mom replied, unruffled by Lo's bad mood. "Is Jazz staying for dinner?"

Lo looked behind her, as if Jazz might have followed her in without her noticing. Nope. No sign of Jazz, who was probably eating exotic flavors of froyo and comparing bra sizes or something equally dumb.

"No. She's not here."

"Oh. Okay." Her mom looked surprised. Not shocking given that Jazz spent as much time at their house as she did at her own. More, probably. Especially after Jazz's mom had taken off with her yoga instructor and left her and her dad on their own a couple of years back.

"Dinner will be ready in half an hour," her mom said, slicing and dicing and julienning.

"All right. I think I'm going to sit outside for a bit."

The backyard was bathed in late-afternoon sunshine. Lo wandered over to the maple tree that stood watch over the house from the back corner of the yard and draped herself heavily in the old tire swing.

I bet Jazz wouldn't be caught dead on the tire swing now, she thought bitterly. She's too busy hanging out with the It Girls and being all mature and stuff.

She remembered when they had begged Lo's dad to hang the swing for them. They had taken turns swinging and spinning on it for hours, screaming into the sky when it spun wildly and giggling when they climbed on it together. Until this summer, when Jazz suddenly decided that they were too old for a tire swing and started worrying more about how she looked than having fun with her best friend.

Lo thought of Jazz walking away with the It Girls without a single look back at her. It had been Jazz and Lo for so long.

Jazz and Lo. (Never Lo and Jazz.)

Always together, so that when Lo walked into a room without her, someone always asked where Jazz was.

Lo wasn't entirely sure who she was without Jazz's shadow to hide in.

TEN

||||||||||||||||||||||||||||||

Six years ago…

Back in the second grade it was a huge deal when a new kid came to school. A new kid broke up the monotony of days filled with dodgeball at recess and what felt like an endless slog of lessons. A new kid meant something exciting was happening for once. Lo heard about the new girl before she even stepped into the schoolyard.

Everyone was talking about her.

Literally everyone.

Lo was curious about this new girl and where she had moved from and what she was like. She secretly wondered if the new girl could possibly become her best friend. She'd never admit it to anyone, but in the deepest, most secret depths of her heart, she had always wanted a best friend.

But Lo was too quiet and shy to make friends easily. And she was definitely too awkward. She was always invited to birthday parties, and she was included in recess games. But she had never had one very best friend she could tell her secrets to or stay up with late into the night, giggling until her father yelled at them to get to sleep. Which is what she figured was exactly what you did when you had a very best friend.

Someone to tell everything to. Someone she could confess her very worst fear to—that, deep down, Lo was afraid she really wasn't very interesting.

The first thing Lo saw when she walked onto the playground was that they had finally put up a new swing. The old one had been broken for months. And the second thing she noticed was the crowd of kids surrounding the new girl, fighting to get her attention.

Her heart sank.

She was too late. No doubt someone else had already claimed the new girl as their best friend. Probably Abbi, who spelled her name with an *i* that she dotted with a little heart. Abbi had shiny blond hair that always looked perfect, and she wore a rainbow sundress that looked brand-new. Lo looked down at her jeans. The ones with the ripped-out knee. She loved them because she could draw on her knee where it was visible through the hole. Today she had drawn a dragon with flames coming out of its mouth.

The new girl was beautiful. She had a cool accent that made her seem mysterious and exciting. She definitely wasn't shy like Lo. She threw her head back when she laughed and told Abbi with an *i* that her rainbow sundress was "absolutely smashing."

"Absolutely smashing," Lo whispered under her breath. It didn't sound nearly as cool when she said it.

At lunch the new girl—Lo had discovered that her name was Jazmin—ate with Abbi and her friends. Lo could hear them laughing from where she sat at her desk in the corner of the classroom. Lo hid behind her library book and watched her.

She felt someone come up behind her.

"Nerd!" Bobby Zucker yelled, grabbing the book out of her hand. "What are you reading, horse face?" She wasn't surprised. He probably couldn't even read, Lo thought, wishing she was brave enough to say that out loud. She looked around for the teacher, but she was on hall duty today and had left them alone after making them swear they'd behave. Apparently Bobby had lied.

Everyone was staring at them, watching Bobby and laughing, like calling her horse face was so incredibly clever. Lo wished the floor would open up so she could disappear and never come back. She felt her face burning and tried to think of something clever to say.

You're a horse face. No. You're a...a fopdoodle! She had read that one in a book once and had always wanted to say it out loud. But Lo said nothing. She just looked at her desk while Bobby waved her book around, a book about knights and kings that the librarian had told her was too hard for a kid in second grade. But Lo had taken it out anyway because she had been reading since kindergarten, and she didn't like being told a book was too hard for her.

Someone suddenly snatched the book out of Bobby's hand.

The class gasped.

"Here," a voice with a mysterious accent said.

Lo looked up.

The new girl was holding the book out to her, smiling kindly at her. "I haven't read this one. Is it good?"

Lo nodded, unable to speak.

"I'm Jazz," the new girl said. She looked down at Lo's knee, showing through the hole in her jeans. "I like your dragon."

And that was how Lo got a best friend.

ELEVEN

"Lo, could you please clear the table?" Lo's mom asked. "I've got a huge case that I really need to do some work on tonight."

Lo's mom was a lawyer. A pretty good one, according to her dad, who proudly bragged to anyone who would listen about all the criminals she'd helped put in jail. She specialized in helping people who had been the victims of predators. For years Lo had thought that meant her mother was fighting off bears and tigers at work, which seemed really cool and exciting. Secretly she was a little disappointed when she found out her mom's job had nothing to do with wild animals.

"What's it about?" Lo asked, only half-listening as she piled the plates on top of one another and then carried them over to the sink, where her dad's arms were plunged up to his elbows in sudsy dishwater.

"It's a sexual-harassment case," her mom said, opening her laptop and settling down in the spot Lo had just cleared.

"Ewww." Lo wrinkled her nose. She didn't want to hear about her mom's sex case. She must have said that out loud and not in her head like she thought she had, because her mom looked up and frowned.

"It's not a sex case, Lauren. It's about a boss who used his authority to treat one of his employees really badly."

Lo cocked her head to the side, looking at her mom with interest. "What did he do?" she asked.

"He touched her inappropriately," her mom said.

"Inappropriately how?"

"He smacked her on her butt. And he deliberately brushed up against her breasts. Things like that."

"That's disgusting!" Lo said. "He's her boss!"

This was the great thing about her mom. She didn't treat her like a baby who couldn't handle grown-up things. If Lo asked a question, her mom always answered.

"You're right. But not just because he's her boss. No one should touch anyone else if they don't want them to."

Lo nodded. "Or say inappropriate things to them," she told her mom.

"Right. No one should say things that make you feel uncomfortable. And they shouldn't touch you either. You always need to say something if anyone makes you uncomfortable, Lo." Her mom was looking pointedly at her over the top of her reading glasses. "They should be teaching kids about consent at school. Not all parents feel comfortable talking about things like this."

"Yeah," Lo agreed. "Definitely not something you have trouble talking about."

"No," her mom said with a laugh. "Maybe they'll talk about it in sex ed. Isn't that coming up?"

Lo shrugged. "I dunno," she mumbled. She was still trying to figure out how she was going to get out of going to sex ed. It was one thing to talk about that stuff with her mom. But talking about it in front of everyone? With her teachers sitting in the room with them? Nope. Lo would rather fight an entire battalion of Cybermen. But something told her her mom wasn't about to let her play sick that day. Especially after this particular conversation.

Dear Doctor,

Did anyone ever talk to you about consent? You know what that is, right? Things seem pretty advanced in the space-time continuum. My mom likes to remind me to speak up for myself if someone makes me feel uncomfortable, and I know that's important. But I couldn't even tell Jazz that she hurt my feelings when she ditched me at the mall! So if someone did do something that made me uncomfortable, would I really be brave enough to say something? I want to be brave. But Jazz is the brave one. I'm just…me. And I'm so used to no one noticing me. Jazz is the star, and I'm just in the background. I wish I was more like you. You're always brave. Were you brave when you were a kid? Do you think that's something you can learn?

I hope so. I really do.

Your friend,

Lo

TWELVE

Lo had walked all the way around her backyard twice.

She had peered into every hiding spot she could think of and moved flowers gently out of the way so she could examine their stems. She had gotten down on her hands and knees and crawled around the back porch. She had actually ventured under it, even though there were cobwebs and spiders under there, and Lo was deathly afraid of spiders. She had watched "Arachnids in the UK" with her hands over her eyes, even though the Doctor was pretty thrilling in that episode.

There wasn't a single chrysalis anywhere to be found.

Lo sat back on her heels and wiped angrily at her eyes. She was *not* going to cry about a stupid chrysalis! Even if she and Jazz *had* found one together every single year for as long as she could remember and watched it change into a butterfly. And now there didn't seem to be even one for her anywhere in the yard, and it totally sucked. She felt like she was losing everything important in her life. She knew it was dumb and that it was just a chrysalis.

But everything was changing.

She was losing her best friend, and without Jazz, she couldn't even find a stupid chrysalis.

She stood up, wiping her hands off on her pants, leaving long streaks of dirt and grass behind. She didn't care. She looked around the yard once more, ready to give up. She tried really hard not to believe that it meant something that she couldn't find her chrysalis. Like her friendship with Jazz literally depended on her finding a chrysalis, and she had failed at both.

She stopped at the tire swing and contemplated climbing on and swinging, even if that made her a little kid. She grabbed the tire and was about to shove it so that it swung away without her when she saw it. A tiny little flash of bright green and gold glinting in the sunlight from the tree branch above.

Dear Doctor,

What's it like to regenerate into a new person? Is it scary?

I figure regenerating is probably a lot like when a caterpillar becomes a butterfly. And a chrysalis is like the TARDIS! You go in, become an entirely new person, and when you come out, you get to start all over.

I wonder if Jazz would like me better if I regenerated into someone more like her and Abbi.

Your friend,

Lo

THIRTEEN

Lo walked into the cafeteria, feeling some of her old shyness and uncertainty creeping back. Normally she'd be sitting with Jazz, but she hadn't even spoken to her since the whole bra thing at the mall. She had texted a few times but got a random response that said *bsy txt ltr*. That was it. So now she wasn't sure where she'd be eating her lunch or where Jazz would decide to plant herself—but she had a sneaking suspicion it wasn't going to be at their usual table. She barely had time to look around the room when Jazz flew across the cafeteria with a little shriek, throwing herself at Lo and nearly knocking her back out through the doorway.

"Lo!" she screeched, sounding more like Abbi with an *i* than like the Jazz she knew. But then, she was Jazzi now, wasn't she? "The It Girls are planning something big!"

"What?" Lo asked, grabbing Jazz's arm to stay on her feet.

"It's huge!" Jazz screamed in her ear. "And they want *me* to plan it with them."

"Okay," Lo said, not sure what this had to do with her.

"They want me to sit with them so we can...you know...plan. Together."

Oh. And there it was.

"You don't mind, right?" She wasn't even looking at Lo. She was looking over Lo's shoulder at the It Girls' regular table, where they reigned in all their perfectly dressed and made-up glory. Abbi had her perfect blond hair perfectly arranged around her perfect face with its perfect smile. She was wearing what appeared to be the It Girls' official uniform of a shirt that hung off one shoulder. On hers was a picture of a blond woman with her hair covering her face that looked startlingly like herself. Lo looked back to Jazz, who was already starting to edge away from Lo and back toward Abbi's table.

Yes! she wanted to scream. *Of course I mind! You're supposed to be my best friend! Why don't you want to hang out with me anymore?*

But she couldn't bring herself to do it, and she forced herself to smile instead.

"Sure. We can catch up later, right?"

"Absolutely," Jazz replied while turning and heading back to her spot at the It Girls' table. "You're the best!" she called out over her shoulder.

Lo watched her go, wanting to call out to her to come back. The It Girls immediately shifted to make space for her and welcomed her to their table like she belonged there. Lo studied her briefly before deciding that she probably did belong with them. Jazz had on ripped jeans that Lo knew had cost her every cent of the birthday and allowance money she had saved.

Her T-shirt hung off one shoulder, showing off the strap of the fancy lace bra she had bought.

Lo sighed. She looked down at her T-shirt, which read *I Think Outside the Box* with a picture of the TARDIS on it. She most definitely was *not* an It Girl.

But Jazz definitely was, which meant Lo would have to either eat her lunch alone or find another table to sit at. Lo turned and looked around the cafeteria, shifting awkwardly from one foot to the other. She stopped suddenly when she realized this made it look like she had to pee. She saw kids she knew, but no one looked up and made eye contact, and there was no way she was going to invite herself to sit at a table whose regulars had been clearly established since school started. Other kids had joined their table sometimes, of course, but Lo knew it was Jazz who got their attention, not her.

She heard a burst of laughter from the It Girls. Jazz and Abbi were sitting with their heads together, looking at something on Abbi's phone. Lo felt her eyes prickle—she was *not* going to cry in the middle of the cafeteria! She swallowed hard and caught Bobby Zucker looking at her, smirking. Of all the people in the cafeteria, the one person to make eye contact was Bobby freakin' Zucker—the worst human being in the school? She was not about to give him the satisfaction of seeing her upset.

Lo shook her head and spun around, almost hitting Jason Lieberman with her lunch tray.

"Oops." He grinned. "Careful with that. You almost decapitated me."

"Then move!" Lo snapped. She pushed past him, dumping her tray and stomping out of the cafeteria. She'd rather do her homework in the library than stand in the doorway of the cafeteria, waiting forever for someone to ask her to sit with them.

FOURTEEN

Lo barely slept that night. The rest of the day had been a blur of trying to look like she wasn't a completely friendless loser who no one wanted to hang out with. She kept her head down in the halls and tried to smile when the kids around her in class chatted together and said something funny—like she was part of it all. But all Lo could think about was Jazz and Abbi with their heads pressed together in a little duo that she didn't fit into.

She lay awake late into the night, staring at the ceiling and watching shadows and wondering where was she going to sit the next day. She knew her classes weren't going to be stressful, because they had assigned seating. But would Jazz meet her at her locker like she usually did so they could walk to the cafeteria together? What if she didn't? Lo definitely didn't want to skip lunch again. Her stomach had growled so loudly all afternoon that Bobby Zucker had called her growly guts in math class and made everyone laugh at her.

So skipping lunch was unquestionably not an option.

The next day Lo headed to her locker as soon as the bell rang before lunch, her stomach clenching. She turned the corner, absolutely sure she wasn't going to see Jazz waiting but hoping with every fiber of her being that she'd be there.

She wasn't.

Lo spent as long as humanly possible putting her books in her locker, but Jazz didn't come.

Crap. She'd have to go to the cafeteria and find somewhere to sit or risk being called growly guts again.

Lo stood inside the doorway like she had the day before. There was Jazz at the It Girls' table, giggling with Abbi and looking completely unconcerned that Lo had been waiting for her. *Fine*.

She had started to check out where other people she knew were sitting when she overheard a bunch of kids at a table to her left talking loudly.

"I swear, if they don't have at least *one* of the Doctors at FanCon this year, I'll scream," one girl was saying to the others. "I'll literally scream!" At least half of her tablemates were reading comics, and not one of them had a bra strap showing. Lo took a couple of steps toward them and smiled shyly. This was definitely a group she could relate to.

"Who's your favorite?" Lo asked, her heart beating wildly. She was willing someone to answer so she didn't feel like a total weirdo standing there with her tray.

"Thirteen! Obviously," said a kid with a huge, unruly mop of brown hair. Lo vaguely knew Zev from her art class. "You?"

"Thirteen for sure. And Ten. Because David Tennant is the best."

"Yes! Thank you! Ten will always be my Doctor," yelled MJ, a girl with blue hair and one side of her head shaved. "Nice backpack," she said, nodding at Lo's TARDIS bag. "Sit. Please. So do you go to FanCon?"

"Of course! And I heard they're showing a preview of the new Spider-Man movie this year," she said, sitting down beside the girl and digging into her lunch. She grinned at the idea that she was talking about Spider-Man with a girl named Mary Jane.

"I'm Zev," the kid across the table said. "My pronouns are they and them."

"Right. Lo. Umm…she/her."

"Cool." Zev nodded, pushing their hair out of their face. "You clearly know MJ, and that's Audrey and Jade," they said, pointing at two girls with their heads bent together over a comic book. Audrey was tiny and pixie-like with cropped blond hair and the coolest purple and pink sparkly eye shadow. Jade nodded at her, pushing jet-black hair out of her eyes. "And that's Jaden, Jade's twin. Which I still think is such a weird name choice by their parents," Zev finished. Jaden had the same black hair falling into his eyes as his sister, and he flashed her a quick smile before looking back down at his phone.

Lo laughed and waved at everyone, and they nodded or waved in return and then dove back into their comics or conversations. But not in a rude way. More in a way that made her feel like they were comfortable with her being there. Like she belonged at their table with them.

FIFTEEN

Lo and MJ were in the same social studies class, so they walked there together after lunch, chatting about their favorite Spidey villains—Lo liked Mysterio best, and MJ loved Doc Ock—and discussing which superpower would be the coolest one to have.

"I think it would be so awesome to be able to fly!" MJ was saying. "Can you imagine how quickly you'd be able to get to school in the morning? No traffic! You could sleep in until the first bell."

"True," Lo admitted. It was an excellent argument.

"And if you passed over someone you didn't like, you could drop stuff on them." MJ grinned.

"Like what?"

"I don't know. Eggs?"

"Why would you be carrying eggs?" Lo asked, giggling madly.

MJ was laughing now too. "I don't know. It was the first thing I could think of!"

"Well, I'd rather be invisible," Lo told her. "How freakin' cool would it be to be invisible?" She saw Jason Lieberman watching them from his locker across the hall. She stuck out her tongue at him, and he turned away, blushing. Lo had no idea why Jazz was so obsessed with him. He was always lurking around, playing with his hair. She turned back to MJ. "If you were invisible, you could eavesdrop on people. You could sneak up on them without them ever knowing you were there!"

"Are you two quite finished?" a voice dripping with icicles called out. Falkenstein! Or, as Lo liked to call her, Frankenstein. She was standing in the doorway to the classroom with that ever-present scowl pasted on her face. "Perhaps you'd like to join us?"

Yikes, Lo thought. Ms. Falkenstein was unarguably the meanest, scariest teacher in the entire school. And she was just about to close the door on them. If you didn't make it to Frankenstein's class *before* the bell rang, she locked the door, and you had to go to the office for a late slip. Lo had tried to reason with her that you weren't technically late until *after* the bell rang—and had ended up in detention for her troubles.

"Yes," Lo told her as Jason Lieberman slipped past her and MJ. "We were just talking about what the best superpower is," she explained.

"Just take your seat, Lauren." Ms. Falkenstein sighed.

"Sorry," Lo mumbled. She sidled past the teacher, followed closely by MJ, who had a hand over her mouth to hold back her laughter.

"Well, class," Ms. Falkenstein began, closing the door in Bobby Zucker's face as he made a desperate run for it just as the bell rang, "if Lauren and Mary Jane are finished their fascinating discussion, perhaps we can get started."

Dear Doctor,

Just when I was having the worst possible day, and Jazz had deserted me AGAIN to go hang out with the It Girls, I found a bunch of kids who don't care what I'm wearing or whether some boy likes them or not. I guess I don't really know them well yet, but they definitely don't judge my T-shirts or think I'm a little kid for liking Spider-Man and <u>Doctor Who</u>. THEY actually like them too! I thought that if I didn't have Jazz, I'd be all alone. But you get that, don't you? You probably think you'll be alone forever every time you lose a Companion. Losing a friend is hard, no matter who you are. Maybe the universe sends people into your life when you need them the most. When you feel the most alone. And with Zev and MJ, I think I feel less alone.

Your friend,

Lo

PS. What do you think the best superpower would be? I think it's definitely invisibility, but MJ thinks it would be better to fly. I guess with the TARDIS, you already CAN fly.

SIXTEEN

Jazz caught a ride to school with Lo like she had for the past few years. It was a lot quieter than it used to be, though, except for her mom's music. While Lo tried to engage her in conversation just to fill up the awkward silence between Beatles songs, Jazz scrolled through Instagram on her phone and sipped a truly repulsive-looking green smoothie she had concocted. Lo watched incredulously as Jazz took a selfie with her smoothie and posted it, like she didn't hear Lo ask about her night.

"See you after school, girls," Lo's mom called out as they grabbed their backpacks and got out of the car.

"Oh, not me," Jazz said. "I'm going to Abbi's after school. Byeeee!" she called over her shoulder.

First I've heard of it, thought Lo as Jazz ran off to find the It Girls. Lo lost sight of her, but she knew Jazz had found them, because she could hear them shrieking at each other from the other end of the hallway.

"Loud, aren't they?" a voice said over her shoulder.

Jason Lieberman.

"I'm surprised you're not right there in the middle of them," Lo replied.

"Really? But my voice is so much lower and more manly," he said, grinning at her.

Lo snorted a reply as she saw MJ and Zev leaning against her locker, waiting for her. She headed over to them, and Jason sauntered off down the hallway.

"Finally!" MJ threw herself in front of Lo, pulling Zev along with her. "We've been waiting forever, haven't we, Zev?"

"Forever," Zev agreed.

Suddenly every single stressful thought Lo had been having, the dark cloud that had been following her all morning, was gone.

"Did you watch *Doctor Who* last night?" she asked, smiling widely.

"Why do you think we're standing around like a couple of Weeping Angels over here?" MJ and Zev struck menacing poses.

"What's your problem, Angels?" Lo asked, channeling the Doctor.

Zev grinned, breaking their very excellent Angel pose as MJ leaped toward Lo.

Kids were staring at them, and normally that would make Lo want to hide. But MJ and Zev were laughing and making scary faces at each other, and suddenly Lo didn't care who was watching.

SEVENTEEN

Lo almost forgot about Jazz deserting her. Almost. She almost didn't remember that they had spent basically every waking—and sleeping—moment together since the second grade. Almost. And she felt good about her new friends and…it all fell apart the second she saw her in the hallway.

"Jazz!" Lo spotted Jazz's newly highlighted hair with the neon-pink streak in the crowd of kids plodding along like a herd of cows past her locker. "Jazz!"

Jazz turned, then elbowed people out of the way to get to her. "Hey!"

Jazz was smiling. That had to be a good sign. Right? It had to mean they were still friends, even though they had barely spoken a word to each other since Jazz had left her hanging in the cafeteria.

"Hi! God, I feel like we haven't talked in *forever*." Lo hated how needy she sounded, but she couldn't stop herself from babbling. "So I thought maybe we could have a sleepover? Like old times," she finished lamely, feeling like she was seven years old again. *What is wrong with me?*

"A sleepover?" Jazz crinkled her nose adorably and tossed her hair over her shoulder. It was a classic It Girl move.

"Well…not a sleepover like a little-kid type of sleepover. Obviously!" (*Lo, stop babbling!*) "A movie night!"

"Oh." Jazz looked slightly more interested, so Lo desperately forged on.

"Right! Like a real girls' night! You can *totally* pick the movie and everything. And we can make your favorite cookies."

Jazz studied her for a second, then smiled widely. "That sounds fun. As long as I *really* get to pick the movie this time."

Lo laughed. "You can pick. I promise."

"Because you always want to watch superhero movies."

Lo stopped laughing. Since when did Jazz *not* want to watch superhero movies? They had spent an entire weekend debating DC versus Marvel. The winner was obviously Marvel. It wasn't even a contest as far as Lo was concerned. No matter how strenuously Jazz had insisted that *Wonder Woman* was the greatest superhero film ever made. Because everyone knew *Spider-Man* and basically all *The Avengers* movies were far superior in every conceivable way. But now was clearly not the time, and she bit back the words bubbling up before they could escape and smiled in a way she hoped looked sincere.

"We can watch whatever you want. I swear."

"Oh, wait." A frown clouded Jazz's face, and Lo felt her heart stop. "I'm busy on Saturday. But I can come on Friday."

"Yes! Friday works! We can definitely do Friday," Lo blurted wildly. She wanted to jump up and down and throw her hands in the air in victory, but she knew Jazz would run for it if she did anything too crazy or dramatic. A *Doctor Who* quote was definitely out of the question too. She pulled in a lungful of air and let it out slowly, trying to calm herself down.

Lo was relieved. She'd win her best friend back with a classic "Jazz and Lo Night of Adventure." Even if the new Jazz didn't seem to like superheroes anymore. Lo found herself hoping the old Jazz was the one who showed up on Friday night.

Jazz was nodding and already looking past Lo toward where the It Girls were congregating near Abbi's locker. "Okay. I'll bring chips."

"Salt-and-vinegar?" Lo asked.

"Definitely."

It was a plan. A solid plan. And Lo was going to make sure everything was absolutely perfect.

EIGHTEEN

"I guess Jazz finally realized what a dork you are." A familiar voice oozed its way across the hall. *Ick. Double ick.* Bobby Zucker. Supervillain and lifelong bane of her existence. But not even Bobby Zucker could ruin her good mood right now. Not when Jazz was going to come over to her house this weekend for a sleepover.

"Oh yeah?" She spun around and almost smacked him in the face with her backpack. Would have served him right too, she thought.

"Yeah. You should just find some other dorks to hang around with."

Lo smiled, channeling the Doctor. "Oh, don't be such a potato dwarf, Bobby," she told him, tossing her bag over her shoulder.

Bobby's mouth opened. Then closed. Then opened as Lo walked away, grinning like crazy because she'd never thought in a million years she'd ever work up the nerve to use that insult on anyone. Let alone Bobby "Potato Dwarf" Zucker.

Dear Doctor,

I have a chance—a real chance!—to fix things with Jazz! She's coming over on Friday, and we're going to have one of our famous sleepovers, and I know she'll remember how much fun we used to have when it was just the two of us hanging out and eating junk food and watching Marvel movies or <u>Doctor Who</u> episodes half the night. If I do this right, I'll have my best friend back, and everything will be the way it used to be. No It Girls. No Jason Lieberman. No bras. Just Jazz and Lo and maybe the sloth onesies. Maybe I can get her to plan a prank with me. Like the time we walked over to Bobby Zucker's house and threw stones at his window until he stuck his head out, and then we fired water guns at him.

Wish me luck!

Your friend,

Lo

NINETEEN

"Welcome!" Lo said dramatically, throwing the door open wide for Jazz. *Welcome?* Jazz had spent at least half of her life in Lo's house. She had her own key and everything. And the best Lo could come up with was *welcome? Not off to a great start here, Lo.*

"Come on in," she said much more casually. "I was just about to put the cookies in the oven."

"Awesome!" Jazz squealed. She squealed a lot lately, Lo noticed. Obviously an It Girl phenomenon. No! She was not going to be critical tonight! Tonight was about getting Jazz back. But…preferably the old Jazz. The Jazz who didn't squeal so much. Or at least so loudly.

She stuck the baking sheet in the oven and set the timer for ten minutes. Jazz followed Lo down the hall politely. Like a guest. Like she hadn't spent countless nights here over the many years they had been friends.

Maybe the cookies will start to make things more like they used to be, Lo thought, leading the way into her room.

"Come on. You can put your stuff in here."

"Hey! You found a chrysalis!" Jazz said, bending down to look at the jar on Lo's desk.

"Yeah. It took forever. It was above the tire swing. You should have seen me climbing up to get it. I almost fell off twice! It's the only one I've seen this year."

"I always love that little gold thread holding it all together," Jazz mused, sounding almost like her old self again.

"Me too."

Jazz walked the length of the string where Lo had pinned up all her favorite photos with tiny wooden clips. She stopped in front of a photo of the two of them at Arts Camp, their faces smeared with marshmallows and chocolate and their arms wrapped tightly around each other.

"I have this one on my mirror," she said thoughtfully.

"I know," Lo said, although it had been weeks since she'd been in Jazz's room, and as far as she knew, her photos had been replaced with pictures of the It Girls.

The timer sounded before they'd even had time to settle in and talk. *Darn.* Just when they had started to reconnect!

The cookies slid onto a plate, leaving a long, thin trail of gooey melted chocolate behind.

"Oh my god!" Jazz moaned, biting into one and closing her eyes dramatically. "I haven't had sugar in days!"

"*What?* Why?" Lo almost yelled. *I mean…come on! No sugar?*

Jazz shrugged. "I'm trying to get abs."

Lo opened her mouth. Then snapped it closed. Nope. Not tonight, Lo, she thought. *But seriously? Abs? Who needs abs when you're only twelve going on thirteen?*

"Well then, you're in luck. I also have cupcakes."

Jazz snickered. She had brought along some romantic comedies, which didn't really surprise Lo. The It Girls all seemed like the rom-com type. But this was supposed to be a classic Jazz and Lo night.

"I actually thought we could watch…" she started to say, but her voice faded off as Jazz stared at her.

"*Doctor Who*?" Jazz rolled her eyes.

"No. Just something fun. Like, *The Mandalorian* maybe?" Who would say no to Baby Yoda? Lo thought.

"You said I could pick the movie." Jazz frowned. "And these *are* fun. They're comedies."

"Right. Yeah, okay. Sorry. Whatever you want," Lo sputtered, trying to backtrack so Jazz would stop frowning.

"Let's just get changed first," Jazz said, sighing. She pulled out her old camp T-shirt and a pair of pink-flannel pajama pants.

Just like the old Jazz, Lo thought, smiling widely. Maybe this could work after all! No, it *was* working!

But before she could comment on it, Jazz pulled her shirt over her head. Lo gaped at her.

"Are you wearing a *water bra*?" she screamed, pointing at the extremely well-padded bra Jazz was wearing and laughing hysterically—half expecting Jazz to laugh with her. But Jazz's face turned fuchsia as she pulled her shirt back on.

"Wait! What are you doing?" Lo asked, the laughter dying in her throat.

"I'm going home. Abbi told me that this was a mistake."

"A mistake?"

Jazz was throwing her things back in her bag violently.

"Jazz, wait. I'm sorry for laughing. It's just…you *have* boobs. You don't need a water bra."

"You're so immature, Lo."

"I'm *twelve*! Jazz, stay. Please. I can make this better! Let me fix it. There's lots more cookies. And we haven't even watched your movie yet!"

Jazz paused in the doorway. "You're almost thirteen, Lo. When are you going to grow up?"

"I'm sorry," Lo pleaded. "Please don't go."

Jazz looked at her but didn't put her bag down.

Lo felt like she was going to throw up.

"Jazz," she said suddenly. "Are we still friends?"

Jazz stared at her but didn't reply. She didn't say yes. Finally she closed her mouth, then opened it again.

"I just don't think we have much in common anymore, Lo."

She turned and left without looking back. Lo watched her leave, wishing that for once she had just kept her big mouth shut.

Dear Doctor,

I messed everything up.

I thought if I could just get Jazz to hang out like we used to, I could show her that nothing had changed. But everything has changed.

And she doesn't want to be my friend anymore.

I've been friends with Jazz for so long that I'm not sure how to not be her friend.

Who am I supposed to be if I'm not part of Jazz and Lo?

I really wish you were real so you could tell me what to do.

Your friend,

Lo

TWENTY

Lo hadn't thought it was possible, but things went sliding downhill from pretty bad to waaaay worse on Monday morning.

Gym had never been her favorite subject unless they were playing dodgeball or capture the flag or something else that required her to use her imagination. Sometimes she could get through an entire game pretending she was the Doctor doing battle with the Cybermen. But they weren't playing in the gym today. Today was *the* day. The *big* one. The Day to End All Days. Today was sex ed day.

Lo had tried everything she could possibly think of to get out of it.

She had "lost" the permission form, but the school had anticipated kids trying this and had emailed copies to all the parents, just in case.

She had told her mom she was sick, but her mom's stupid saying "No vomit, no fever, no day off" meant she and Jazz were dropped off at the doors to the school promptly at eight forty-five, just like every other day. Jazz beelined straight inside without her.

And to add to her utter humiliation, her mom waited until she actually went inside to drive away. As if Lo was going to mutiny and make a run for it or something. And based on the fact that she had been complaining about it for a solid month, that was a distinct possibility. But there she was, dumping her bag in her locker and trudging to the gym.

Just in time for sex ed.

"At least they separated us from the boys," MJ whispered, linking arms with Lo. "Not all schools do that."

"Can you imagine?" Lo whispered back, letting MJ drag her through the doorway.

"Zev tried to sneak out and hide in the bathroom, but they got caught and now they have to sit in the front row. They tried to argue that being nonbinary should mean they can choose which group to join, but no one would let them come sit with us."

"That's so not fair!" Lo frowned.

"Okay, quiet down, please," Miss Simms called out. "Today we're going to talk about menstruation."

"Oh dear God," Lo whispered to MJ. "Can you just shove me into a wall or something so we can get sent to the office?"

"Lauren, do you have something you want to share?" Miss Simms asked.

For one brief, horrifying moment, Lo thought the teacher was asking her if *she* got her period.

"Oh. No. Sorry. Carry on," Lo said.

MJ stifled a laugh.

For the next hour Lo learned everything she never wanted to know about periods, sex and masturbation. She spent the entire time wishing she had a TARDIS she could disappear into and fly away to another moment in time and space. Literally anywhere other than here in this exact moment. When it was finally over, she grabbed MJ's arm and pulled her toward the door.

Where Miss Sims was standing, handing out condoms from a basket like the worst loot bags in the history of the world.

"Oh my god. Get me out of here!" Lo hissed.

"Here you go," Miss Simms was saying. "Better safe than sorry, ladies."

Lo tried to avoid her gaze. She tried to sidle past without Miss Sims noticing. She tried to will herself invisible to get out the door undetected. She wished in vain for a natural disaster to suddenly occur.

"Here, girls." Miss Simms thrust a handful of condoms at them.

"No, thank you!" Lo pulled MJ, who was giggling madly, away and through the door.

"God, that was a nightmare," MJ said.

"I seriously thought she was going to tackle us and force a bunch of condoms into our hands," Lo agreed. "We're twelve! Who has sex at twelve?"

"I'm thirteen." MJ shrugged. "Actually, I think it's pretty responsible of them. I mean, *I'm* not about to have sex, but if I were, I wouldn't want to get pregnant."

"Me neither," Lo admitted.

"And my brother's best friend had sex when he was our age. At least, that's what he told my brother."

Lo just shook her head. She couldn't even imagine being ready for sex at her age. But then, most of the time she couldn't imagine being ready to grow up at all.

"And honestly," MJ continued, "if she said the word *menstruation* one more time, I was going to have to fake a brain aneurysm or something."

Lo giggled. "I know, right? Doesn't the school realize we have the internet if we want to know this stuff?"

"Right? Although be careful what you google. For real. You can't unsee some of the stuff I've googled by mistake. God. Listen…" MJ pulled Lo over to her locker. "Do you want to come over this weekend and watch movies or something? We can get the new Stephen King movie and watch it in the dark." She shivered deliciously.

"Seriously? Yes! I love Stephen King!" Lo smiled.

"Awesome. I'll text you my address."

"Cool!"

Lo waved and ran to her math class just as the bell rang.

She realized suddenly that she hadn't thought of Jazz all morning.

TWENTY-ONE

In fact, she didn't really think about Jazz at all until she walked into the cafeteria for lunch and happened to glance over at the It Girls' table purely by accident.

There was a group of boys hanging around the table, as usual. But this time they were playing keep-away with a bunch of white balloons and making loud comments for all their friends to hear.

"Someone grab a bottle of water so we can have a wet T-shirt contest!" one boy shouted.

"Are you wearing a thong?" another asked one of the It Girls.

"Hey, Abbi! Does the carpet match the drapes?" one boy asked.

Lo wasn't entirely sure what that meant, but judging by Abbi's face, *she* did.

"Jazz, if I told you you have a good body, would you hold it against me?"

Lo knew what *that* meant.

She frowned and shook her head, remembering what her mom had told her over dinner that time. How no one should be allowed to say anything that makes you feel uncomfortable. She watched the It Girls for a minute. They definitely looked uncomfortable. Abbi had a fake smile plastered on her face that looked like it was literally causing her pain. But Jazz wasn't smiling. She was looking down, her face a scarlet mask of humiliation.

Lo knew that look.

Jazz was about ten seconds from bursting into tears.

Lo shook her head. *It's none of your business, Lo,* she told herself. *She doesn't even want to be your friend anymore. Why do you even care?*

But deep down Lo knew she'd care no matter who was being harassed. No one deserved to be treated like that. The fact that it was Jazz just made it a million times worse. Because no matter what they were going through, Jazz had been coming to her rescue since the day Bobby Zucker called her horse face.

The kids sitting around the It Girls were watching intently, like it was the latest Avengers movie. Some were laughing, and not one of them said a word to the boys cavorting around them like they were there just to entertain them all.

Don't get involved, Lo told herself, sitting down across from MJ and pointedly ignoring the commotion across the room. "Those guys are such idiots." She took a bite of her sandwich, trying not to look at them and failing miserably.

"I know, right?" MJ rolled her eyes.

"They're total jerks," Audrey said from behind her book. She was sitting at the other end of the table. Jade and Jaden nodded in agreement.

"And where did they get those stupid balloons?" Lo ranted.

"What balloons?" Zev asked, swiping a fry from MJ's tray.

"The balloons they're hitting people in the head with," Lo said, watching the boys fling the balloons at each other and laugh like a bunch of hyenas.

"Lo. Those aren't balloons. Those are the condoms from sex ed," MJ told her.

"No…they're…" Lo felt the words die on her lips. *Oh god.* The boys had blown up their condoms and were batting them around like balloons. They were laughing like it was the funniest thing in the world. She saw Bobby Zucker tap his condom balloon on Abbi's shoulder, who tried to ignore it. But how do you ignore a blown-up condom in your face?

Out of the corner of her eye, she saw Jason Lieberman, his face scarlet, looking absolutely mortified. She heard him say, "Come on, guys, leave them alone," but no one was listening. He was the only one. Out of every single person in the cafeteria, not one other person had spoken up. Lo looked for a teacher, but whoever was on duty today had disappeared. Typical. Never around when you needed them. She watched as one of the boys held his "balloon" in front of him and made a lewd gesture with it at Jazz.

Nope. That was not okay.

She stood up without a word and made her way over to the It Girls' table.

"Where's she going?" Zev asked.

Lo didn't catch the answer. She was already across the cafeteria, her eyes narrowed as she approached the It Girls' table.

"Show us your bra, Jazz," one of the boys—Bobby, of course—was saying. "Is it lace? Come on. Just a quick look. All the girls do it," he leered. He ran his hand down Jazz's back and snapped her bra strap.

Hard.

Jazz screamed.

Without thinking, without even considering the consequences, without wondering how he'd react, Lo marched up to Bobby, reached down and gave him a wedgie so hard that she yanked four inches of his underwear up out of his pants.

"How do *you* like it?" she asked.

Dear Doctor,

You are not going to believe what just happened...

TWENTY-TWO

"You did *what*?"

Lo had to hold the phone away from her ear so that her mother's voice didn't completely deafen her.

"I gave a boy a wedgie?"

"Why would you do that, Lo? What could possibly have made you think that was a good idea?"

"I didn't really give it a lot of thought first, Mom," Lo told her.

Her mom snorted. "Well, that's glaringly obvious, Lauren."

"The boys were saying gross things to the girls and asking to see their bras!"

"What? Did they touch them?" her mom asked, switching effortlessly into lawyer mode.

"No. They just…hit them with blown-up condoms." Words Lo never thought she'd have to say to her mom.

There was a short pause. "Okay, that's it. I'm coming down there."

"No! Jeez, Mom. You'll make it worse!" Lo hissed into the phone, turning away to avoid the prying eyes of the secretary, who was being extremely unsubtle about trying to listen in.

"How could it possibly be worse, Lauren?" her mother demanded.

"I can handle this, Mom! Everyone always wants me to grow up and then don't actually *let* me! I'm not a little kid, and I can handle this."

Her mother was silent for a second. Probably because she was used to swooping in and rescuing her every time she got into trouble. Lo might not actively *want* to grow up, but she wasn't a baby anymore either. And she didn't want anyone rescuing her like she was some princess in a fairy tale.

"Are you sure, Lauren?"

"Yes." Out of the corner of her eye, Lo saw the secretary waving at her. "Look, Mr. Cohen is here. I have to go."

She hung up before her mother could ask more questions. Lo shuffled into the principal's office behind the secretary and sat down, trying not to make eye contact. She could have sworn she saw the secretary hiding a smile as she closed the door behind them.

But she'd probably imagined it, given the thunderous scowl on Mr. Cohen's face. *Yikes.*

"Would you like to explain what happened?" Mr. Cohen asked, tenting his fingers in front of himself and staring at her over the top of his glasses. She figured it was supposed to make him look serious and smart. Lo thought it made him look kind of douchey. Although arguably not as douchey as the motivational posters he was famous for decorating his office with. She particularly hated the one of the kitten hanging from a branch, which read *Hang in there*. The cat was about to plummet to his death, for crying out loud!

Mr. Cohen cleared his throat, pulling Lauren's attention away from the dreaded poster.

"Well?"

"I gave Bobby Zucker a wedgie."

"And may I ask why?"

"I gave him a wedgie because he was harassing my friend." *Well, former friend.*

"Isn't giving someone a wedgie harassing them?"

Lo tilted her head and frowned. *Crap.*

"Yeah. Probably," she admitted. "But it wasn't any worse than what he was doing to her." Definitely not her strongest argument. But he had a point she hadn't actually considered.

"And what exactly was he doing…" He glanced down at her file. "Lauren?"

Lo sighed. Then realized suddenly that Bobby wasn't in the office too.

"Wait. Why isn't Bobby here?" she asked, looking around like he might be hiding behind one of Mr. Cohen's ridiculous posters.

"Because Bobby is the injured party."

"What?" Lo exploded. "Are you kidding? He was making comments—inappropriate comments! About the girls' bodies.

And asking to see their bras! And blowing up condoms like balloons. He snapped Jazz's bra, so I gave him a wedgie. He sexually harassed her, and for some reason, *I'm* the only one in here! I may deserve to be here, but so does he."

She crossed her arms over her chest and sat back, breathing heavily. Let him punish me, Lo thought. She probably shouldn't have grabbed Bobby's underwear—which felt *disgusting*, and there wasn't enough hand sanitizer in the entire world to ever make her feel clean again—but he shouldn't have been touching Jazz or asking to see her bra. The Doctor wouldn't have stood by, and neither could she.

"You've never been in trouble before, Lauren. So I'll let you off with a warning."

Lo watched as Mr. Cohen wrote something in her file before standing up to dismiss her.

Oh, hell no, Lo thought.

"And what are you doing about Bobby?" she asked, meeting his eyes for the first time since walking into his office.

"What do you mean?" he asked.

"I get that I did something wrong, but I'm not the only one who should be sitting in here. Is he getting off with a warning too? And what about the boys who were making those gross gestures with their…their balloon wieners!"

Mr. Cohen stared at her. Lo had never, ever stood up to a teacher before. She felt like she was floating near the ceiling and just watching this new, badass version of herself challenging the principal.

"So...you're accusing Bobby Zucker of playing with balloons?" Mr. Cohen asked dimly.

"No, sir. I'm accusing him of pretending a blown-up condom was his penis and...and...*thrusting* it at the girls." Lo could *not* believe she'd just said *penis* to the principal!

"Well...I'll...I'll handle it," Mr. Cohen stammered before standing up and ushering her out, his face red.

"But—" Lo started to protest. *Bobby and his creepy friends should get expelled!* But before she could say anything, Mr. Cohen had closed his office door and shut her down.

We'll see, Lo thought, taking a late slip and heading to class. *We'll just see about that.*

Dear Doctor,

You'd be so proud of me! I stood up for the It Girls when no one else did! They were being sexually harassed, and I walked right over and…well, let's just say I defended their honor. It doesn't matter how. But I'm the only one who got in trouble. The boys got away with it. And it's not right.

There's got to be something I can do to make it right. You'd never let them get away with it. I don't think I should either. So I made a list of things I can do.

Move all the principal's office furniture into the cafeteria so he has to sit there and bear witness to what the hyena boys do to the girls at lunch.

Paint Bobby Zucker's locker with feminist graffiti and Fight the Patriarchy stickers.

Make condom balloons and tie them to Bobby Zucker's locker. Between all the girls, we probably have at least a hundred from the sex ed talk.

Tape a sign that says "My name is Bobby Zucker, and I am a Neanderthal who treats girls like trash and thinks condoms are balloons" to Bobby's back.

It's a start.

Your friend,

Lo

TWENTY-THREE

"Lo?" Jazz was waiting in the hall. Her face was still kind of pink, but she looked much calmer than she had when she was being attacked by Bobby Zucker.

"Yeah?"

"I just—I wanted to say thanks. For what you did. To Bobby," Jazz said, scuffing the toe of her wedge sandal on the floor.

Lo nodded. "It's okay," she said.

"I know things aren't the same with us." Jazz glanced up at Lo, then back down at her perfectly pink, manicured toes.

"No," Lo agreed. "They're not."

"Look, you didn't have to stick up for me. But I'm really glad you did. No one else did."

"Yeah. Well…except for Jason Lieberman. He tried to get them to stop," she admitted grudgingly.

"Really?" Jazz's cheeks blazed. "Well, I guess I'll see you around?"

"Okay."

Jazz nodded and started heading away from her.

"Hey, Jazz?" Lo called out.

Jazz turned, tucking a piece of hair behind her ear.

"Is it really worth it? Being popular?"

Jazz shrugged before heading back down the hallway to her friends.

TWENTY-FOUR

The first thing Lo did when she got home from school was check on the chrysalis. She liked to look in on her to see if she was changing color in her little sleeping-bag cocoon. There were always weeks of anticipation, waiting for her to break free and emerge a butterfly, and watching for any tiny, minute changes.

Lo looked in the jar and thought her eyes were playing tricks on her. She didn't see it at first. She turned the jar around, thinking idly that maybe the chrysalis was on the other side. But the stick it had been hanging on was empty.

"No!" Lo cried. The cocoon had somehow come loose and was lying on the bottom of the glass.

She opened the jar, reached in and picked up the delicate, feather-light cocoon. Carefully. So very, very carefully.

"It's okay," she whispered, terrified she was going to crush it. "It's going to be okay. I promise."

She gently set the cocoon on a clean dish towel and then looked through the kitchen drawers.

"Come on, come on!"

She rifled through pens, batteries, old receipts, elastic bands and odds and ends collected over years.

Finally, at the back of the drawer, Lo found what she was looking for.

"Yes!" Lo ran back to the cocoon, the tube of superglue in her hand. "It's okay," she crooned to it. "I'm going to take care of you."

She pulled the stick out of the jar and dabbed on a thick glob of glue. As gently as possible, she picked up the cocoon and held the little stem at the top against the glue as she counted to sixty. Then counted two more times. Three minutes. She counted twice more, just to be safe. Five minutes. Gently, slowly, Lo let go of the chrysalis, now stuck back on the stick.

"Okay. That's good. See? I told you you'd be okay."

She put the stick back into the jar and watched, chin resting on her arms, waiting to see if the glue would hold. Waiting for a sign that the sleeping creature inside would be all right and hoping with all her might that she had fixed it.

Dear Doctor,

Do you believe in reincarnation?

I guess you must, since reincarnation is pretty much the same as what you go through when you regenerate. I'm waiting and watching to see my caterpillar turn into a whole new creature. If I managed to save her, she'll come out of her chrysalis a butterfly, with her whole life ahead of her. She'll have to get used to being a butterfly, I guess, and make new friends and everything. But do you think it's possible that she'll be happier as a butterfly? And will she forget what it was like being a caterpillar?

I guess what I want to know is, when she leaves everything behind and becomes someone else, does she miss her old life? Or does she start over and forget everything from her past?

Thanks for listening. Even though MJ and Zev are cool, and my mom is actually pretty awesome, sometimes I feel like you're the only one I can really talk to without worrying I sound like a little kid.

Your friend,

Lo

TWENTY-FIVE

"I don't want you to think it's okay to give people wedgies, Lauren," Lo's dad told her later over a plate of turkey meat loaf, carrots and mashed potatoes smothered in a thick, rich gravy.

"I mean, if they'd kept their sexist comments and their hands—and their *condoms*—to themselves, I wouldn't have had to," she said.

Her dad choked on his potatoes, and Lo smacked him on the back to help them go down. "You okay?" she asked. He nodded and gulped down his water without meeting her eyes.

"Well, I'm proud of her," Lo's mom said. "I mean, I don't want you giving people wedgies as a rule. Touching someone else without their consent isn't okay, Lauren. But you stood up for your friends. I just wish you could have found a better way to do it."

"I know." Lo nodded. "And I get that touching him was not only incredibly disgusting but was wrong."

Lo's mom snickered in response.

"I'm proud of you too," Lo's dad said. "I don't know why the boys thought that kind of behavior was all right. It must have made the girls extremely uncomfortable. I'm glad you stood up for your friends."

"They're not really my friends," Lo told him.

"That's even harder than standing up for someone who *is* your friend," he said.

"Yeah. I guess. Anyway, I won't do it again."

"Good. Okay then."

Lo caught her dad glancing weirdly at her mom. What was that all about?

He picked up his plate and edged toward the door to the living room. "Anyway. So I'll just go see what's on TV," he said, backing away slowly.

"What's up with him? Midlife crisis?" Lo joked.

"What? No!"

She giggled. "Am I finally getting that baby brother I've always wanted?"

"Of course not!" Lo's mom looked horrified.

"Okay, okay. What is it?"

Lo's mom took another forkful of salad and smiled at her. *Jeez. What was she going to say?* Her mom put her fork down and reached over, pushing a piece of hair behind Lo's ear. "Well, you know your body is changing..."

Oh god. Lo didn't like where this was going.

"MOM! I already know about sex, okay? I literally *just had* sex ed, and I think it may have scarred me for life, so can we seriously not have this conversation? Please?" Lo felt her neck getting hot.

"It's not about sex, Lo. But you know you can ask me anything you want about that, right?" Her mom smiled gently.

"I know, Mom. Jeez!"

"Good. But that's not why I wanted to talk to you. Not about sex, anyway."

Lo felt relieved but confused. "Then what is it? I said I know it was wrong to touch that idiot, and I won't do it again. I understand consent works both ways."

Her mom sighed. "It's not that—although I'm glad to hear you say it. The thing is…I think you need to start wearing a bra."

How did her mom find it so easy to talk about bras and sex? Lo's face was on fire. She'd rather be talking about literally anything else.

"I don't want to wear a bra, Mom. I don't need one." Lo crossed her arms over her chest and arranged her face in an expression she fervently hoped showed that the subject was most definitely closed. She looked at her mom, who was smiling softly at her now.

"I know you don't want to grow up, Lo. But it's happening whether you want it to or not. And I know you're uncomfortable talking about this, but you shouldn't be. I'm not. We should be able to talk about anything without being embarrassed. Especially things that happen to every single woman." She studied Lo for a second, then stood up. "Okay. I know it's easier said than done." She took her plate to the sink, which meant Lo could escape this horrific conversation. She made a break for it while her mom's back was turned and fled to her room.

There was a shopping bag waiting on her bed from Justify—the same store she had gone to with Jazz.

Oh god. She already went out and bought me bras. Please don't let them be lace! And for the love of all things holy, do not let there be a water bra in that bag!

She picked up the bag as if it contained dynamite and could explode at any moment and tipped it over so the contents fell onto her bed.

Sports bras.

Exactly the same as the one Lo had tried on. No lace or satin or fluorescent color in sight. And not a single water bra either, she noticed with relief. She didn't feel remotely ready for all of this growing-up stuff, but her mom was right. It was starting to happen whether she wanted it to or not. And at least her mom understood her.

TWENTY-SIX

Lo stared at herself in the mirror, turning one way and twisting around the other way, trying to see if she could tell she was wearing a bra.

Nope.

She couldn't see it. Unlike Jazz's crazy water bra, the sports bra actually helped hide the curves that Lo wasn't quite ready to embrace or, God forbid, show off.

She threw a baggy sweatshirt over her T and headed to school.

In the hall, Lo was terrified someone could tell. She kept her head down, just waiting for someone to yell out, "Hey, everyone! Lo is wearing a bra! Look at her!"

But it didn't happen.

"Hey! Lo!" MJ grabbed her arm as she walked past and pulled her over. "Where are you going?"

Lo crossed her arms over her chest. "Umm…gym?"

MJ looked at her oddly. "Are you okay?"

"Fine!" Lo yelled. "Sorry. I'm fine. Absolutely awesome. I have to go. I don't want to be late for gym!"

"Okay. Well, wait a second and I'll come with you." MJ slammed her locker door closed and followed Lo down the hall, keeping up a steady stream of chatter about some new horror show on Netflix. Lo threw open the door of the changeroom and slipped inside.

Oh crap. Lo had totally forgotten she'd have to undress in front of everyone. How exactly was she going to manage this?

Lo tried to wedge herself inside her locker to change.

It didn't work.

She managed to jam about half of her body into it before she got stuck and MJ had to pull her back out.

"What are you even doing?" MJ asked.

"I just…I wanted to see if I could fit. Haven't you ever thought about that?" There was no way she was about to admit the truth. That she didn't want anyone watching her change.

"Ummm…I guess so," MJ admitted, lacing up her running shoes.

Lo tried taking off her T-shirt and removing it under her hoodie, but she got tangled up, and MJ had to help her free herself again. Even MJ, who was up for anything, was starting to look confused. Lo tried just turning her back on the rest of the room. It almost worked. Until Abbi saw her and screamed so loud that people on the second floor had to have heard her.

"Oh my god! Are you wearing a *sports bra?*"

Lo stopped moving. No. Abbi couldn't be talking about *her*, right? There were lots of other girls changing. There was no way Abbi was talking about her. Abbi never even noticed she existed most days. She was definitely talking about someone else. And she was in gym. There were probably lots of girls wearing sports bras, right?

"Lo! Hey! I'm talking to you!"

Okay. Maybe she *was* talking about her.

Lo turned slowly. Her face was burning. It felt like it was on fire. Literally.

"Yeah?"

"Oh my god! It *is* a sports bra! That's, like…*so* adorable!" Abbi crowed with laughter, standing in her lace push-up bra and pointing at Lo like she was some kind of freak. "Hey! I think my little sister has that bra. She's nine."

"Leave her alone, Abs." Jazz appeared out of nowhere and stepped between Abbi and Lo. "Come on. We're going to be late."

"Whatever." Abbi pulled on a T-shirt, snickering but not saying anything else.

Lo caught Jazz's eye and nodded her thanks. It was nice to know that even if she wasn't her friend anymore, Jazz still had her back. At least when it came to Abbi with an *i*'s weird need to make Lo feel like she was a little kid who didn't belong.

Dear Doctor,

Jazz defended me! Against the It-iest of all the It Girls! Abbi with a freakin' i̲. It has to mean something, right? It has to mean that no matter what's going on between us, we're still friends.

It just has to.

Your friend,

Lo

TWENTY-SEVEN

"Oh god. If there is anything worse than dodgeball, I don't know what it is," MJ moaned to Lo.

"I like it," Lo whispered back. "But having to stand around while the popular kids pick teams made up solely of their equally popular friends before they get stuck with the rest of us sucks."

"And then getting picked last!" screamed MJ. "That's definitely the worst!" She twined her arm through Lo's and led her onto the field.

"Is there a problem, Mary Jane?" Miss Simms called out.

"No. Well, yes, actually." MJ stood up straight and squared her shoulders. "It's just that the teams always end up exactly the same because the captains are always the same people."

Lo gaped at MJ, who seemed perfectly at ease challenging the teacher.

"Okay. Why don't you be a captain today then?" the teacher said, and winked.

"Awesome!" MJ high-fived Lo and marched to the center of the group. "I pick Lo!"

Like some kind of hero out of a...well, out of a comic book, MJ picked every single girl in the class who usually got chosen last.

"Well, this is an odd team," said a girl named Miranda, who was clutching an inhaler tightly in one hand.

"We're a group of stone-cold weirdos and I love it!" MJ crowed. "Now are we going to win?" she yelled.

"Absolutely not!" Lo shouted back.

"No way!" Miranda laughed, taking a hit off her inhaler.

"Then let's go out there and not care how it turns out but have a freakin' awesome time together!" MJ boomed, holding out her hand so the girls could high-five her as they ran past.

"Good job, Captain," Lo told MJ, slinging an arm across her shoulder and leading her out onto the field.

TWENTY-EIGHT

"Did you hear?" MJ asked, throwing herself down at the lunch table beside Lo and pushing Jade's tray over to make space. "Sorry, Jade."

"Did I hear what?" Lo asked, spearing a cucumber with her fork.

"Yeah, what?" Audrey called out from her usual spot at the end of the table. Audrey usually wore black, but she had mixed it up today by adding a hot-pink, sparkly fun-fur vest. Lo thought it looked pretty amazing.

"About the party!" MJ waved to get Lo's attention.

"Ummm...what party?" She crunched on her cucumber and waited for MJ to get to the point while she wondered idly how she'd look in a fun-fur vest.

"Abbi's party!"

Lo laughed. "Abbi isn't about to invite either of us to a party, MJ."

"Yeah, this table is not getting that particular invitation."

Audrey pulled her book back in front of her face as Jade and Jaden nodded. Lo realized she had never heard Jaden actually speak. He whispered to Jade a lot. And she usually answered for him. *Huh.*

"Oh my god, Lo. Are you listening to me? She's inviting the whole class!" MJ paused dramatically before blurting out, "Not just the popular kids. Everyone! And that means this table too!" She looked pointedly toward Audrey.

"Seriously?" Jade asked.

"Yes! They're sending out an e-vite tonight."

Lo shrugged.

"Don't you want to go?" MJ asked. "I know your whole thing with Abbi and the It Girls, but it might be fun."

"No. Not really." Lo wrinkled her nose.

MJ looked at her pleadingly. "Lo, we have to go. Everyone will be there. Like, literally *everyone.* And I'm dying to see what her room looks like. Do you think everything in it is pink?" MJ asked eagerly.

"Probably. And covered with weird fur and glitter."

"Hey!" Audrey looked down at her vest.

"On you it looks amazing," MJ told her. "But imagine a whole room of that."

"Oh. Yeah. Weird." Audrey nodded.

"See? Come on, Lo. You can't say no to that!" MJ begged. "Zev. Back me up!"

Zev, who had been ignoring the conversation until now, looked up from their Miles Morales comic. "Well, I could definitely say no to the company of Abbi and the rest of the group. But I did hear there's going to be a sundae bar and a chip truck."

"I didn't hear that!" shrieked MJ.

"We did." Jade and Jaden nodded at them.

"Lo! There's no way we can miss this!" MJ said firmly.

Lo glanced over at Abbi's table, where Jazz was whispering something to Abbi, who was giggling at their little secret.

Jazz was one of the It Girls, so she'd definitely be at Abbi's party. Maybe this was Lo's chance to prove she wasn't a little kid anymore. If she could just show Jazz that they weren't so different, maybe they could be friends again.

Lo nodded. "Okay. Count me in."

"Yes!" MJ yelled. She started running through everything she owned and planning her outfit out loud while Zev vetoed most of her suggestions.

"Well, what are you wearing?" she asked them after Zev dismissed the tenth outfit suggestion.

They shrugged. "Easy. Dark-wash jeans and my green T-shirt. I look awesome in that shirt."

Lo half-listened, wishing silently that Jazz would realize they could still be friends, despite their differences, and then wondered idly why she still cared so much.

TWENTY-NINE

"What are we talking about?" a voice asked, as someone threw himself down with great enthusiasm beside Zev.

Ugh. Jason Lieberman.

"What are you doing here?" Lo asked, frowning.

"What do you mean?" Jason plopped an order of fries down on the table and pushed it toward Zev, who grabbed one and stuffed it into their mouth hungrily.

"Yum!" They smiled happily.

Traitor, Lo thought.

"Aren't you worried the It Girls will see you sitting with us and revoke your popularity card?"

"What are you talking about?" Jason laughed, taking off his hoodie and draping it over the back of his chair.

Ugh. He literally looked like he'd walked into American Eagle and just bought whatever was on the mannequin in the window. No personality at all, Lo thought, looking down at the vintage Beatles shirt she had borrowed from her mom's closet.

"I'm talking about you taking over our table with your stupid fries." Lo looked around the table for support, but even MJ was looking at her like she was crazy.

"Lo, I've been sitting here forever. Yeah, I sit over there sometimes, but I always come back here. Zev has the best comics in the entire school!"

"Why, thank you." Zev half-bowed and grabbed another fry at the same time.

Lo looked at MJ, expecting her to laugh and deny that Jason Lieberman and his dumb perfect hair had ever sat with them, but MJ was reaching for his fries too.

"Well…you haven't…I mean, *I* haven't seen you here before!" she said, feeling really, really lame.

"I've got soccer practice at lunch usually, but they're moving it to after school now, so I get to hang out here. And speaking of which, when did *you* start hanging out at *our* table?" he asked, smirking.

"Me?" Lo sputtered. "I've been here…I don't know…I didn't even…"

"Okay, okay." MJ waved her arms in front of them. "Time-out. Truce. Whatever. There's room for both of you at *my and Zev's* table. Right, Zev?" She winked at them.

"Absolutely. And we do accept bribes for priority seating," they said, pulling the plate of fries closer.

"Hey!" Jason laughed, then turned and started asking Zev about the latest comic-book releases from Marvel, ending the conversation.

Lo watched and wondered how she had never noticed that Jason Lieberman—soccer star, undisputed cool kid and apparent reader of comic books—could move so easily between the It Girls' table and their little corner of the cafeteria.

THIRTY

Lo's computer dinged as she was finishing up her math home-work. The e-vite to the infamous party, no doubt. It sounded like a death knell to Lo, who really, *really* didn't want to go to Abbi's stupid party. Even if there *was* going to be a sundae bar and a chip truck.

She took a deep breath and clicked on the email.

COME TO OUR TOTALLY AWESOME PARTY!

The words emblazoned across the screen were in Comic Sans capitals. Which to Lo looked exactly like someone yelling. And seriously? Comic Sans?

Typical, Lo thought, remembering Abbi's annoyingly shrieking, cartoonlike voice in the changeroom. She looked at the picture on the invitation.

The It Girls, their arms wrapped around each other, with Jazz right in the middle beside Abbi. Lo sighed. If she was going to get her friend back, she might as well start with Abbi's dumb party.

"Mom!" she called out, half-hoping her mom wasn't home. "Can I go to a party?"

Dear Doctor,

Do you get invited to many parties?

I hate to admit it, but I don't. I think the last real party I went to was a birthday party that the whole class was invited to. Honestly, that's the kind of party this one is too. A "whole class is going so we may as well include you" invitation to a party I don't even want to go to.

A party where Abbi and her minions will hang with the popular kids and ignore the rest of us.

And I REALLY don't want to go to a party with the popular kids. I'll probably end up standing against the wall awkwardly or something.

But what would you do? Would you go if you thought it might bring your best friend back?

Your friend,

Lo

THIRTY-ONE

"What should I wear?" MJ asked. "Zev was no help at all." They had gone to MJ's house to prep for the party. She was yanking clothes from her closet and tossing them onto the bed with impressive speed and dexterity. Shirts, pants and something peach-colored and lacy that looked suspiciously like a bridesmaid's dress landed beside Lo.

"Jeans?" she suggested. She pushed a sequined skirt off her lap.

"Jeans? No one is going to be wearing jeans!"

"I'll be wearing jeans," Lo said. "So will Zev. What else would everyone be wearing?"

"I don't know! I thought it might be dressier." MJ bit her lip and stared at the pile of clothes surrounding Lo.

"Wait. Why would it be dressier?" Lo asked. She didn't own anything fancy except a dress her mom had bought her to wear to a wedding the previous year. And she was pretty sure no one would be wearing anything like that.

"I don't know. It *is* Abbi with an *i*," MJ argued.

"Yeah, I guess. Well, I'm still wearing jeans." Lo shrugged.

MJ gave in. "Okay. But I'm only wearing jeans if I can find a cute top to go with them." She dove back into the depths of her closet. Shirts came flying out at a blistering pace. Lo tried to catch them but was soon covered in a thin layer of cotton and polyester.

"What about this one?" Lo held up a T-shirt with a rainbow unicorn on it.

"Lo! We're not ten."

"Yeah, yeah. How about this one?" Lo held up a red T-shirt with a banana on it.

"Why would I wear a banana shirt?" MJ asked.

"Haven't you learned anything from the Doctor? You can't go to a party without a banana!" Lo grinned.

MJ laughed. "Gotta love the Doctor." She turned back to her closet. "What about this?" She held up a tank top.

Lo studied it thoughtfully. "Yeah, okay. That looks cool."

"Yeah?"

"Absolutely."

"Lo?" MJ was avoiding eye contact, her cheeks red.

"Yeah?"

"Do you think they're going to have…kissing games at the party?"

Dear Doctor,
KISSING GAMES?

THIRTY-TWO

Lo hadn't seriously believed there would be kissing games at Abbi's party. She thought they only did that in old books and movies about teen parties. So she didn't actually expect it. At least, not until she walked into Abbi's basement and saw Abbi and the rest of the It Girls hanging around the snack table. They were eyeing the boys like they were made of chocolate, and giggling like maniacs. They were all overdressed, as far as Lo was concerned, wearing what she knew Jazz would call "cute" dresses—too short for Lo's taste, with little tiny straps. MJ was going to kill her.

Lo couldn't see Zev, but Jade and Jaden were sitting on a loveseat, watching something on Jade's phone. She had somehow lost sight of MJ, so Lo tried to look casual and not at all like she would rather be anywhere other than Abbi's basement, where people might be expected—no, *encouraged*—to kiss each other. Lo's heart sank. Jazz looked up and met her eyes. Lo smiled. *Please don't make this weird, please don't make this weird!* Jazz nodded and smiled a little before Abbi shrieked something in her ear, and the moment passed.

Lo did not belong here.

Her mind spun desperately. Maybe she could fake a sore throat. Or diarrhea. Or say there was a family emergency, and she had to go home. There was absolutely no way she was going to kiss some sweaty boy in Abbi's dimly lit basement with K-pop playing in the background.

"I can't believe Jason came."

Lo heard a familiar voice behind her. She thought for one heart-stopping second that Jazz was talking to her. Then she heard Abbi respond.

"Of course he's here! Everyone's here."

"Do you think he knows I like him?" Jazz asked her.

"He will after tonight," Abbi said, giggling.

Lo rolled her eyes.

"Do we even have a bottle?" Abbi asked.

Lo smiled at the floor and felt her pulse return to normal. *Yes!* No one had glass bottles anymore. Everything came in cans or plastic. And no one played spin the can! She tried to paste a look of deep regret on her face in case Jazz was looking but found herself smiling instead.

"I can't believe so many girls are wearing dresses! Wait. What are you smiling about?" MJ asked, handing her a cup of fruit punch.

"I'm just…having fun," Lo replied. She caught a glimpse of Jazz over MJ's shoulder. Jazz was frowning.

"We need a bottle!" Jazz shook Abbi's arm frantically. She looked panicked.

"We don't have one," Abbi told her.

"Well, you must have something!" Jazz was desperate now. *Desperate for a stupid kissing game!* She looked around wildly. "Wait!"

Jazz dove across the room, pulling down a vase of silk flowers from a shelf.

It looked like a vase.

It had to be a vase.

Oh god.

Lo sighed.

It wasn't a vase.

Jazz pulled the flowers out of the cobalt glass bottle and waved it above her head. Victorious. The room erupted in giggles from the girls and cheers from the boys as Lo wilted visibly. There was still time to fake an emergency. She grabbed her phone, ready to pretend she had gotten a text from her mom demanding her immediate return home, but MJ grabbed her hand.

"Don't even try it," she said, "or they'll all think you're a baby. And you're not leaving me here alone."

She pulled Lo into the middle of the room.

"Are we playing or what?" Jazz called out.

THIRTY-THREE

The lights went off suddenly, plunging the entire room into darkness. A few people screamed. Others giggled nervously.

This is it. This is how I die. I am literally going to have a heart attack in Abbi's pitch-black basement waiting for what has to be the worst, most horrifying party game ever.

Someone lit a few candles, and the room glowed with a golden flickering light. MJ sat, pulling Lo down with her. She landed hard. Gracelessly. Right beside Jazz, who was perched prettily beside Abbi. Lo tried to rearrange her limbs into some semblance of casual elegance and ended up with her legs tangled together and her hands settling like lumps in her lap. Within seconds everyone in the basement was sitting in a circle.

"Let's do this!" Bobby Zucker called out, smacking his rubbery lips that had probably never seen a tube of lip balm in his life. He had so much product in his hair that it was standing straight up and looked like a nuclear blast wouldn't ruffle it.

Nope.

No way.

If she had to kiss Bobby Zucker, she would puke on his shoes.

"Who goes first?" someone asked.

"It's my party. I'll go," Abbi said, reaching for the bottle.

"No! It should be a boy," Jazz told her.

Lo looked desperately around the candlelit room. It was almost dark enough for her to sneak out.

Almost.

Abbi leaned forward, glancing around the circle. "Okay. Jason. You go."

She pushed the bottle across the circle at Jason as Jazz blushed and hid her face in Abbi's shoulder. They both giggled as Jason reached out and spun the bottle.

Around and around it went, passing Lo once. Abbi and Jazz shrieked adorably as it passed them. It spun again.

Twice. *Don't land on me. Don't land on me,* Lo chanted in her head.

Three times. *Don't land on me!* Lo held her breath, willing the TARDIS to appear and take her away. *If you were ever going to appear, Doctor, this would be an awesome time,* she silently prayed. She noticed Jazz out of the corner of her eye, holding her breath too. But Lo knew with absolute certainty they weren't wishing for the same outcome. The bottle spun again, wobbling slightly.

Until it came to a dead stop right in front of Lo.

Her mouth dropped open.

Jazz's mouth dropped open.

Abbi's and MJ's mouths dropped open.

Jazz leaned over toward Lo. "Ummm…I think it's pointing at me," she said loudly, struggling to be heard over everyone screaming.

"No it's not. It's pointing right at Lo! Go get her, Lieberman!" Bobby Zucker brayed, smacking Jason on the back.

Go get her? Lo most definitely did not want to be "got."

"Kiss her, kiss her, kiss her!" everyone was chanting. Jazz looked like she wanted to smash the stupid bottle on the floor and stab Lo with it.

Lo tried to protest as Jason looked at her, his face pink. He looked at the floor, and she saw him try to hide the fact that he was wiping his hands on his jeans. *Gross!* She did not want Jason Lieberman's sweaty hands anywhere near her. And she absolutely did *not* want to kiss him. She had to do something! She had to stop this from happening, but everyone was watching and she didn't know what to do. He shifted to get to his feet and stumbled a little. Just fall! Lo thought desperately. *Now! Right now! FALL!* She didn't wish a massive head injury on him or anything. Maybe just a twisted ankle or a sprained wrist or something. Anything that would keep him firmly on his side of the circle and away from her. But he got to his feet and walked/stumbled over to her, and Lo felt her mouth flood with saliva. She was going to throw up. She was literally going to puke on someone's shoes! This wasn't right! She thought desperately about what her mom had talked to her about. What they had *all* heard in health class.

"No!" she screamed. The room fell absolutely silent except for the sound of her heart thudding in her ears. "I'm not doing it!"

"Ohmygod. Don't be such a drama queen. It's just a kiss. Stop being a baby!" Abbi tossed her hair.

"I'm not being a baby. And I don't consent to this." Lo crossed her arms over her chest.

Jason looked absolutely relieved. Which, truthfully, she was a little insulted about but also really glad. He didn't even pause. Just turned and plopped himself back down in his spot.

"Okay." He nodded at her and smiled crookedly. "That's cool."

"No, it's not okay!" Abbi leaped up. "This is my party, and she's ruining it! It's a game!"

"But it's a game forcing two people to kiss," Lo argued. "And maybe they don't want to but they're too afraid to say anything."

"No one is being forced," Jazz said through gritted teeth.

"Are you going to ask each person if they consent when it's their turn?" Lo asked. "And what if they feel like they have to consent because everyone is watching? It's just…it's not right." Lo's face was burning, but she felt powerful. She didn't want to kiss Jason Lieberman, and she wasn't about to let anyone make her.

"Actually I don't want to play either," MJ said. She nodded at Lo. "I don't give my consent to be kissed."

Jason stood up. "I'm getting a drink," he announced. Before he had taken two steps away from the circle, every other boy was up and following him across the room to the refreshments.

"But I thought we were going to play!" Abbi whined. "If Lo wants to be a baby, she doesn't have to play."

"Nah," Jason said, stopping and smiling at Lo. "Lo's right."

Lo found herself smiling back at him. She couldn't believe it. She had stood up for herself and for everyone else in the room who didn't feel comfortable with the kissing game, and at least two people agreed with her!

Jazz stood up and stormed past, hitting Lo with her shoulder.

"You ruin everything," she hissed as she ran from the room.

THIRTY-FOUR

Lo searched all over the house for Jazz, but she couldn't find her anywhere. She was ready to give up when she saw a flash of movement outside the sliding glass doors leading from the kitchen to the backyard. Lo slid the door open and stepped outside, pulling her hoodie tightly around her against the brisk night air.

"Jazz?"

Jazz looked up, her face streaked with tears. "Oh, this is just perfect," she snapped. "What do *you* want?"

Lo shrugged. "I just...I don't know. Are you okay?" she asked.

"What do you care? Just go away!" Jazz sniffled, wrapping her arms around herself.

She had to be freezing in that little dress. Lo thought about offering Jazz her hoodie until Jazz yelled "Go!" at her again. Lo nodded, turning to open the door. She paused before going inside.

"Okay. Fine. I was just worried about you." She looked around. "No one else came to check on you, Jazz," she said quietly. The last thing she wanted to do was kick Jazz when she was down. But Abbi with an *i* wasn't out here to see if her "best friend" was okay. Lo turned back to the door.

"Lo, why did you have to come?" Jazz called out.

Lo stopped and stared at her. "I didn't want to."

"Then why did you?" she spit back.

"Because…" Lo mumbled.

"Why, Lo? If you hadn't come, no one would have cared about the stupid game."

"Are you serious? They *should* care!" Lo stared at her, eyes wide.

"Why? What's the big deal?"

"It's a big deal because no one should kiss someone else without their consent, Jazz!"

"Oh my god! You were the only one who didn't want to play! That *is* consent!"

"Maybe. Maybe not. But no one else was going to admit it if they didn't want to play. It's no different from when Bobby snapped your bra strap. That was wrong, and so was this."

Jazz studied her for a minute, then sighed. "No one asked you to interfere in *any* of this, Lo."

Lo glared at her. She was absolutely furious suddenly. "Do you really think I'd do that to you? Let some guy humiliate you like that in front of the entire cafeteria? And anyway, do you really think I wanted my first kiss to be like *this*? With a boy I don't even like in front of the entire class in Abbi Rosenwald's basement? You don't know me at all, do you?" She turned and stalked back into the house, slamming the sliding door closed behind her on Jazz's shocked face.

Dear Doctor,

I honestly thought that out of everyone at that party, Jazz would understand it's not okay to kiss someone who doesn't want to be kissed. I'm not an idiot.

I know it's just a game, and maybe they really were showing consent just by playing. But if Jazz and I were still friends, would I have stood up in front of everyone and said I didn't want to play? Probably not. I would have just done whatever Jazz told me to do. I wonder how many other girls there—or boys— didn't really want to play but felt like they had to? I did the right thing. I know I did.

I just wish Jazz knew it too.

Your friend,

Lo

THIRTY-FIVE

Lo went back to the party. Mostly because MJ was still there, and she was sleeping at Lo's place that night. When she got inside, it was like nothing had ever happened. The boys were playing some dumb game at the food table that involved flipping a plastic cup and getting it to land on some pre-approved spot. And the girls were draped over the furniture, watching a movie. *Titanic*. Definitely old-school but still one she loved. But Lo didn't feel like sitting with the girls. She had, if she was being honest, expected more of the girls to agree with her about the game. That someone other than MJ would have had her back. Well, MJ and, apparently, Jason Lieberman.

She walked to the edge of the room and studied the books on one of the shelves. She pulled *The Three Musketeers* off the wall and opened it.

"Have you read that?" a voice asked. Jason Lieberman had somehow sidled over without her noticing.

"What? Oh. Hey." Lo pushed the book onto the shelf and then pulled another out. "Yeah. My dad read it to me."

"Yeah, my moms read it to me too. Ma always falls asleep when she reads, so Mom would have to take over." He grinned.

"Uh-huh," Lo said, nodding and wondering why Jason Lieberman was talking to her and not one of the It Girls like Jazz or Abbi.

"So listen. What you said during the game was cool. About consent?" He squinted at her.

"Oh. Right."

"My moms talk about consent with me. And you were right. I didn't feel great about that game either, but I don't think I was brave enough to actually say anything." He smiled. "So I'm glad you did."

Lo's mouth fell open.

"Really?" She stared at him. "Thanks. I thought I'd ruined it for everyone." She couldn't have been more surprised by this conversation if Jason had told her he was a Companion and had spent the last year traveling through time and space with the Doctor.

Jason glanced over at Abbi and Jazz, who were watching this exchange with their heads pressed together. "Nah. I'd rather eat Cheetos any day."

It struck Lo that Jason was saying he'd rather eat Cheetos than kiss her, and that was definitely more funny than insulting. Because as nice as he seemed to be, she'd rather eat Cheetos too.

"Flamin' Hot?" She grinned.

"Oh, for sure. I like your shirt, by the way. Ten is my favorite Doctor."

"Ten is—wait. What? You like *Doctor Who*?" Lo squeaked. "I didn't think you'd be into that kind of stuff." Jason Lieberman definitely did *not* strike her as the kind of guy who liked *Doctor Who*. Or, well, *anything* Lo considered cool.

Jason cocked an eyebrow at her. "What does the Doctor say about thinking? Something about it just being a fancy way of saying you've changed your mind." He grinned.

Oh. My. God. Jason Lieberman was a massive geek. Sure, Lo already knew he read comic books. But this was so far beyond what she had ever thought Jason would be like, it actually made her speechless.

"What are you talking about?" MJ wandered over with Zev trailing behind her. "I was just filling Zev in on all the drama."

"We had dinner late, and my dad wouldn't drive me over until I finished. I can't believe I missed Lo lecturing everyone about consent," they cackled.

"I did not lecture!" Lo insisted. "I merely informed."

Zev shook their head. "Not what I heard."

"Well, that's about all you missed," MJ said mournfully. "I really thought an It Girls party would be way more exciting."

"I didn't," Lo told them.

"Audrey did," Zev said. "She was ready to beg her parents to cancel their trip to Cancun so she could come. I'm gonna text her and let her know she's better off on the beach."

"Why don't you all come over tomorrow?" Jason asked, looking right at Lo.

"Ummm…what?" she stuttered.

Jason blushed. "All of you! We can watch *Doctor Who*, and my moms always order pizza on Sunday."

"You had me at pizza," Zev said, nodding.

"You had *me* at *Doctor Who*!" MJ high-fived Jason.

All three turned to look at Lo.

"Well?" Jason smiled. "You in?"

"Oh. Umm…"

"Come on, Lo!" Zev pleaded. "You have to come."

"Well…"

"She's coming," MJ assured them. "Right, Lo?"

"Um. Yeah. Okay. I guess I can come."

"Cool! I'll wear my bow tie," Jason said.

"You do not have a bow tie!" Lo laughed.

"Of course I do. Bow ties are cool," he said, raising his eyebrows in what was clearly his best Matt Smith/Eleventh Doctor impression.

Dear Doctor,
Is this what a crush feels like?

THIRTY-SIX

Lo was tired. Possibly more tired than she had ever been in her entire life. Bone tired, her grandma called it. But MJ wasn't tired at all. MJ wanted to stay up and talk. And what MJ wanted to stay up and talk about was Jason Lieberman.

"He likes you," she squealed at Lo for the millionth time.

"I don't think so, MJ," Lo said, also for the millionth time. "I think he was just being nice." Who thought she'd ever say *that* about Jason Lieberman?

"Come on, Lo. It was so romantic, the way he had your back like that. Like a movie." She sighed.

"A random boy agreeing with me about consent is like a movie? What movies have *you* been watching?" Lo wrinkled her nose.

"He's not some random boy! He's Jason Lieberman! Everyone likes him. He's popular and smart and he's nice. Which is more than I can say for most of the boys at school," MJ insisted. "*And* he's a *Doctor Who* fan! Now who saw that plot twist coming?"

"I know," Lo agreed. "Definitely a plot twist worthy of the Doctor."

"Do you like him now?"

"What? No! I just…can we just go to sleep now? Please?" Lo begged. She wasn't sure she was ready to admit that he wasn't nearly as bad as she had always thought. He was even kind of cool. Not popular-kid cool but nerdy-kid cool. Which was the best kind of cool, in her opinion.

MJ rolled over. "Fine. But…do you think he's going to ask you out now?"

Lo threw the comforter off and leaped out of bed. "I'll be right back. I have to pee," she called over her shoulder, escaping into the hall.

But she walked past the bathroom and into the kitchen, where the chrysalis sat in its glass jar. That stupid party had ruined any chance she had of being friends with Jazz again. After the way things had gone, Lo thought it was possible Jazz might never speak to her again at all. Lo turned on the kitchen light and stared at the chrysalis.

It wasn't green with gold thread anymore.

The chrysalis had turned completely black.

Dear Doctor,

I think I killed it.

The chrysalis, I mean. That sounded way more ominous than I intended.

And probably my friendship with Jazz too. But if I'm being honest—really honest—I think I'm trying hard to hang on to someone who isn't the same person anymore. Jazz isn't that kid who stood up for me in the second grade now. She's changed.

Maybe I've even changed too.

And I'm not sure our friendship can survive.

Your friend,

Lo

THIRTY-SEVEN

Lo almost turned around and ran back to her dad's car before anyone had time to answer the door. What was she doing at Jason Lieberman's house?

Before she could make a decision, the door opened.

"Hi!" A woman as blond as her son, wearing a baseball cap and a pair of paint-spattered overalls, opened the door. "You must be Lo. Everyone else is already downstairs."

"Umm, yeah. I'm Lo," she repeated.

"I'm Lily. Jason's mom. Watch yourself on your way in. I picked a dumb time to paint the hallway. Just don't brush up against anything."

"I won't," Lo promised. The hall was a deep purple color, which looked really cool.

"Jason told us about what you said to everyone at the party last night," Lily said, closing the door behind Lo. "That must have been a really scary thing to do—standing up in front of all those kids."

"Lo's pretty brave." Jason had appeared behind his mom. "Come on downstairs. Zev and MJ are already here."

"Oh, okay. Nice to meet you." Lo smiled at Jason's mom.

"You too. Your ma ordered the pizza, Jason. I hope vegetarian is okay with you, Lo? I think we also got plain cheese."

"Sure. I'm fine either way. Thanks." She followed Jason down the stairs. "I didn't know you were a vegetarian," she told him.

"I'm not. My moms are, and they do the shopping. But they don't care what I eat when I'm out."

"Oh. That's cool. Hey." MJ and Zev were playing a very energetic game of air hockey at a table in the corner. The basement was everything you could ever want in a rec room. A huge TV and the comfiest-looking chairs Lo had ever seen. There was the air-hockey table, plus a pinball machine, a dartboard and an arcade game across from it.

"Do you want something to drink?" Jason asked. He was standing in front of an open fridge that was fully stocked with every kind of drink you could possibly imagine. Juice boxes, cartons of chocolate milk and about a dozen types of soft drinks.

"No, thanks. Your basement is awesome!"

"Yeah. Thanks. My moms wanted me to have somewhere to invite friends to hang out." He grinned at her. "I was really shy when I was younger."

"*You* were shy?" Lo had a hard time believing it.

He shrugged. "I was. Hey, Zev, do you need a refill? MJ?"

"I'm good," Zev called out.

"Me too," MJ said.

"Pizza's here!" a woman called out as she came down the stairs.

"Thanks, Ma." Jason stood up and took a couple of pizza boxes from her—she was a dark-haired woman in workout clothes and a head wrap. "You already know Zev and MJ. This is Lo."

"Hi, Lo. It's nice to meet you." She smiled, showing dimples.

"It's nice to meet you too. Thanks for the pizza."

"Our pleasure." She gave a wink and headed back up the stairs.

"It's starting!" MJ yelled from the sofa.

The next hour was a blur of pizza, cheering, yelling at the screen and high-fiving one another.

"That was awesome!" MJ sighed as the credits rolled.

"Yeah. I miss Matt Smith, though," Jason said. "My moms bought me the boxed set before it was all available to stream, and I loved his seasons."

"WHAT?!" Lo, MJ and Zev all yelled at once.

"But Thirteen is amazing!" Lo argued.

"*And* she's the first female Doctor!" MJ added.

"She's groundbreaking!" Zev said.

"I know. I agree. But I really liked his hair." Jason grinned.

"So…you miss his hair?" Lo rolled her eyes.

"He's got cool hair!" Jason shrugged.

"Ohmygod, you have his haircut!" Zev screamed, pointing at Jason.

"You do!" MJ yelled, collapsing against Zev's shoulder.

Jason looked unbothered. "Do I have an awesome haircut? Yes," he said. "Did I show my barber photos of Matt Smith when I got it cut? Also yes."

"Honestly, there are worse people you could have chosen to be your fashion icon," Lo told him.

"Exactly." He smiled.

THIRTY-EIGHT

Lo felt the change in the air the second she walked into school the Monday after Abbi's party. Something was definitely up.

She trudged down the hall toward her locker. Same as always, except that she usually passed by virtually unnoticed. But today it felt like everyone was turning to look at her.

Of course they're not looking at you, she told herself.

"Did you hear?" someone whispered as she passed.

They could be talking about anything. Stop being so paranoid!

"I heard she absolutely ruined the party," someone else said.

So much for it not being about her. Lo kept walking, the back of her neck itching with the feeling that everyone was watching her.

And Lo absolutely hated being watched.

Lo sensed the It Girls coming before she actually saw them. A hush fell over the entire hallway, and it felt oddly like a cold wind blew in with them, even though that only happened in the movies.

Lo gulped. Literally gulped. The It Girls were strutting down the hall, the five of them in a row so that anyone trying to walk to class had to leap out of their way or squeeze up against the lockers to avoid being run down by them.

It was like something out of one of those teen romance movies Jazz liked so much.

Jazz.

And there she was, sashaying down the hall like she was on a runway in Paris. As Lo watched, Jazz tossed her hair over her shoulder and pretended she wasn't aware that every eye was on her and her friends.

In just a few seconds they'd pass her, and that moment would tell Lo everything she needed to know. How much had Jazz changed? Was their friendship really and truly over? Was Jazz going to talk to her? Would she nod at her as she passed, like she had been doing for weeks? Raise an eyebrow? Throw a punch? Lo braced herself for whatever was to come, ready to respond no matter what. Like Amy Pond, she was ready for anything.

But Jazz swept past her without even a glance. She walked past the locker that until recently she had always dumped half her books in, like she had forgotten it was even there. Like she had forgotten that Lo was even there.

Who cares? Lo thought, tilting her chin up. *Not me.*

Lo shrugged and pretended she didn't see Jazz either as Jazz walked past staring straight ahead, laughing at something Abbi had whispered in her ear. Pretending Lo didn't even exist.

Dear Doctor,

Have you ever felt invisible?

Of course you haven't. You're the Doctor!

When Jazz and I were friends, I always let her decide everything for both of us. She decided what movies we watched and which Doctor Who episodes were best and what costumes we'd both wear for Halloween. Or to FanCon. Remember when she wanted to dress as Ten—MY favorite Doctor—and demanded that I dress up as an Adipose? Her idea. Even though I had worked so hard on my costume. She wore it instead and convinced me to wear the stuffed monstrosity she had created but then didn't want to wear. Then she decided we should take dance lessons instead of the art class I was absolutely dying to take, even though I'm a total klutz. Jazz was always in the spotlight. And I was always somewhere in the wings.

Invisible.

But maybe I'm sick of being invisible. Maybe I want people to see me for once.

Your friend,

Lo

THIRTY-NINE

"Well, *that* was brutal." MJ had crossed the hall from her locker, where she had apparently witnessed Lo's humiliation. "Are you okay?" She was wearing a pink sweater in the exact same shade as her freshly dyed hair and a pair of black jeans with pink roses embroidered on them, tucked into Doc Martens. She looked awesome, but Lo was too shaken to compliment her.

"Yeah." Lo pulled her books out of her locker. Her heart was still beating hard and her throat felt tight, but she was done chasing after someone who didn't want to be her friend. She took a deep breath and smiled at MJ. "I'm fine. Thanks."

And she was, she realized on her way to her chemistry class. She and Jazz had been best friends—inseparable—for so long, she had kind of overlooked the fact that Jazz hadn't always been a good friend to her. But Lo, eager to keep her friend happy and avoid fighting, had kept her mouth shut.

Even when she was afraid of roller coasters but got on the Death Drop at the exhibition because Jazz called her a chicken. She'd ridden it with her eyes shut, screaming the entire time, and then couldn't get the deep-fried Mars bar she had been dreaming about all day because she was 97 percent sure she would throw up if anything passed her lips.

Or when Matt Smith *and* Karen Gillan were at FanCon the previous year and Lo waited in line for two hours to meet them, shaking, absolutely trembling with excitement, while Jazz wandered around shopping. She'd come back and joined Lo in line just as she made it to the front and then taken up their precious face time with the Eleventh Doctor and Amy Pond talking about Karen Gillan's outfit. Lo had almost cried and had clutched her autographed photos to her chest as they walked away, furiously trying to figure out what to say to Jazz to show her that she had seriously *ruined her life*! But then a completely oblivious Jazz had turned to her and said, "You would look amazing in her sweater, you know. You look just like her." How could she be mad after a comment like that?

There had been good times too. Times when Jazz did have her back and was the best friend you could hope for. But right now, seconds after being completely ignored by her, Lo couldn't think of a single one.

FORTY

Lo slid into her seat in chemistry class, right behind Jazz's, where she had always sat. Jazz didn't look at her. Didn't even acknowledge her. Just like in the hallway.

And you know what? Lo was sick of Jazz calling all the shots. She was sick of Jazz being the boss. She was the one who'd decided Lo wasn't grown up enough for her. She was the one who'd decided to drop Lo for the It Girls, and Lo had quietly gone along with it. But for once Lo wanted—no, *needed*—Jazz to know how she felt.

Lo cleared her throat.

Nothing.

She coughed.

No reaction.

"Hey, Jazz?" she said.

Jazz tossed her hair but didn't turn.

"Fine," Lo whispered. "But you're being a real jerk, Jazz."

Jazz whipped her head around so fast she looked like an owl. "Seriously? *I'm* a jerk?" she hissed.

"Yes!" Lo shot back. She saw Jason Lieberman watching them out of the corner of her eye, a concerned look on his face.

"*You okay?*" he mouthed.

She nodded.

"All right, everyone. Open your books to page eighty-nine, please."

Jazz sent her death-ray gaze at Lo and then turned back around. Lo had never stood up to Jazz before. It had actually felt pretty good. Lo opened her book, deciding once and for all that she was just as done with Jazz as Jazz was with her.

FORTY-ONE

The bell rang shrilly, signaling the end of class. The end of a friendship too, Lo thought bitterly.

She gathered up her books, stuffing them into her backpack. She had planned to run for the door ahead of Jazz, but she had draped her hoodie over her chair, and it was hopelessly tangled up in the legs of her chair.

She yanked. And pulled. And tugged. It wasn't graceful. But finally the hoodie came loose.

Lo was about to shove it into her backpack when she glanced up and saw Jazz getting out of her seat.

Lo gasped.

Oh god.

Jazz had a red stain spreading out over the seat of her pants.

Lo knew immediately what was happening, but it was pretty clear that Jazz didn't.

Without thinking, without even considering the fact that they weren't even really friends anymore, Lo leaped over her desk and, in one smooth motion, tackled Jazz, wrapping her hoodie around her waist.

"What are you doing?" Jazz asked furiously, trying to twist out of Lo's iron grip. "Lo, get the hell off me!"

People were starting to stare, and Lo felt it for the second time that day—the horrible prickle she got when people looked at her. Lo absolutely *loathed* being stared at. She literally had nightmares about it. But this was an emergency.

"Trust me," Lo muttered, hanging on to Jazz desperately.

"What?"

"Jazz, for once in your stubborn life, just trust me!" Lo hissed.

Jazz stopped struggling and studied her face wordlessly. Lo tried to indicate how serious this was by scowling as hard as she could at Jazz. She squinted and tried sending a subliminal message—*Let me help you!* She must have succeeded, because Jazz nodded suddenly.

"Fine."

Lo tied her hoodie firmly around Jazz's waist. "There. Just come with me, okay?"

She slung her backpack over her shoulder and led Jazz out into the hall, glancing back at her to make sure the hoodie was staying firmly in place and trying to look like absolutely nothing out of the ordinary was going on.

"Are you going to tell me what you're doing?"

"Not yet," Lo answered, trying to appear casual but fairly sure she looked like she was about to rob a bank.

She grabbed Jazz's arm and pulled her into the nearest bathroom. Thankfully, there was only one other person there.

Lo smiled tightly at her and leaned casually against the wall while keeping a hand on Jazz so she wouldn't bolt. It was like wrangling a ferret. Jazz pulled, but Lo held her arm stubbornly. Jazz shook Lo off as the girl washed her hands and left.

"Well?" she demanded, brushing the imagined wrinkles off her sleeve dramatically.

Lo rolled her eyes but pushed her annoyance away. Now wasn't the time.

"You got your period," Lo told her.

"What are you…? How could you possibly know that?"

"Jazz, *that's* why I put my hoodie around you."

Lo tried to get the point across without coming out and saying it. She raised her eyebrows and nodded dramatically downward.

Jazz looked puzzled. She'd never been very good at charades. Lo sighed, realizing she'd better just come out and say it.

"Your pants, Jazz," she said finally. "You have blood on your pants.

Understanding flooded Jazz's face. "Oh my god!" she shrieked. "Did everyone else see?" Jazz's eyes were filling, threatening to overflow. She pulled the hoodie off and twisted around, standing on her toes to look at herself in the mirror. "Oh god! Does everyone know? Did they see?" She sounded hysterical, but Lo couldn't blame her. If *she* got her period in front of everyone, she'd convince her parents to relocate them to another country. Maybe Costa Rica. She'd always wanted to go there. Or Mexico. "Lo!" Jazz sniffed.

Right. Focus.

"I don't think so. I was right behind you, and I moved pretty quickly," Lo said.

Jazz was crying quietly now.

"I can't believe this is happening!" she sobbed.

FORTY-TWO

"It's no big deal," Lo lied, trying to make her feel better.

"How is getting your period in front of everyone not a big deal, Lo?" Jazz cried. "It's humiliating."

"No one saw! I'm almost 100 percent sure of it," Lo told her. She *wasn't* sure. Not at all. But admitting that to Jazz was definitely not going to make her feel any better. She was about 80 percent sure anyway. Maybe even 85.

"Almost? What do I do? I wasn't expecting it yet. I don't have anything with me," Jazz said mournfully.

Lo looked around the room. "Isn't there a machine or something? For pads?" she asked.

"A machine? Have you ever seen a machine in here?"

"You know I've never had my period! How would I know where the machines are? I thought all schools had them!" Lo snapped. And while she was thinking about it, when had *Jazz* started getting her period? Because she had never mentioned it to Lo. Must have been after she jumped ship and ran off with the dumb It Girls, who probably talked about periods all the time.

Lo shook her head. This wasn't about her. Jazz needed her help, and no matter what had happened, she was going to be there for her.

Lo thought. She had definitely seen a machine somewhere in the school.

"Isn't there one in the first-grade bathroom?" she asked Jazz.

"I don't know! Why would *they* need it?" Jazz was getting a little frantic.

"I think it used to be a senior hallway. I'm not sure. I'll go check. Do you have a quarter?"

"For what?"

"The machine, obviously!" Lo took a deep breath, trying hard to be patient.

Jazz shook her head, her eyes filling with tears again.

"All right, don't panic. God, this is ridiculous," Lo said. "What are you supposed to do if you don't have a pad?" She sighed. "Stay here, and I'll go borrow a quarter from someone for the machine."

"Don't tell anyone what it's for!" Jazz said.

"Right. Because I'd really go up to someone and say, 'Hey, got a quarter for a pad?'"

She left Jazz in front of the mirror, straining to see the extent of the damage to her clothes.

FORTY-THREE

The first person Lo saw was Abbi.

Nope.

Not even if she were the last person on earth.

She sidled past.

"Where *is* she?" Abbi was whining to her friends. "She's making all of us late for class. I *hate* being late!"

Lo had no doubt she was talking about Jazz, but she wasn't about to tell her that she was currently hiding out in the bathroom, looking like something out of a horror movie.

She turned the corner, eager to get away from the It Girls, and ran smack into Ms. Falkenstein's chest, so hard that she bounced off. The teacher reached out and steadied her.

"Going somewhere?" she asked coldly.

"Ummm…yes?" Lo extricated herself from Frankenstein's talon-like grip. "I'm going to the bathroom."

Ms. Falkenstein frowned. "The bell rang moments ago, Lauren. Get to your class. Now."

"Yes, ma'am," she said. And then Lo ran for it, putting as much distance between herself and Frankenstein as possible. She slowed as she turned the corner, breathing hard.

"You look like you're trying to outrun a horde of zombies," a voice called out.

"Hey! Marika." Lo walked over to a girl from her drama class. Marika had jet-black hair, wore black eyeliner and played the drums. Lo thought she was pretty much the coolest girl in their school.

Marika raised an eyebrow at her. "What's up? I assume it's not *really* zombies."

"No. No zombies. Ha. Umm…do you have a quarter I could borrow?" Lo asked.

"Sure." Marika nodded, digging in her pocket and handing her a coin.

"Thanks! I'll pay you back tomorrow," Lo called over her shoulder.

She booked it over to the first-grade hallway, praying she wouldn't run into a nosy teacher. She got lucky. Everyone was in class now, so Lo managed to get to the bathroom without being seen.

She walked in and glanced around quickly. *Yes!* Mounted on the wall was the elusive big metal box. Lo almost skipped over to it, she was so relieved. She slid Marika's quarter in, turned the lever and…nothing. Lo jiggled the lever. She twisted it back and forth. She bent down and tried to look up into the machine, sticking her hand into the slot at the bottom. Lo shook her head, slipped her quarter back out and left, weaving through the deserted hallways. She stopped to check each bathroom on the way back to where Jazz was waiting for her, but every single machine was empty.

Jazz was nowhere to be seen when Lo walked into the bathroom.

"Jazz?"

"Lo? Is that you?" a quavery voice said.

"Obviously." Lo rolled her eyes.

"I didn't want anyone to walk in and see me," Jazz said, poking her head out of a stall. "Did you get a quarter?"

Lo nodded.

"Well?"

"The machines are empty."

"The first-grade bathroom machine?" Jazz asked.

"All of them."

Jazz gaped at her. "Well, *now* what am I supposed to do?"

Dear Doctor,

(mental note to be written down later...)

I'm trying so hard to be more like you. Smart. Brave. Good under pressure. The person you'd want on your side in a crisis.

I think your former best friend being stuck in the school bathroom after an unexpected period disaster counts as a crisis, don't you?

I don't have any idea what to do, so I'll just take a deep breath and think, What would the Doctor do? And maybe yell "allons-y." I've always wanted to find myself in a situation where that would be appropriate, and I think this is it.

Your friend,

Lo

FORTY-FOUR

"Lo, what do we do?" Jazz's voice was getting squealy.

"I don't know!" Lo told her. "I'm thinking."

"Well, are you sure you looked in all the bathrooms?"

Lo stared at her. "No, Jazz. I forgot the hidden bathroom that requires a map and a secret password."

"Well...okay. But you're sure?"

"Yes! I'm not an idiot, Jazz," Lo told her. "I swear I looked everywhere."

"So what do I do?" Jazz was pulling at her hair, something she did when she was super stressed-out.

"You've had your period before. Don't you keep stuff in your locker?" Lo asked.

"I thought I had another week," Jazz said (rather defensively, Lo thought). "I was going to bring pads from home, but I figured I had a few days." She glanced at Lo. "I forgot," she admitted.

"Seriously? Did you listen at all in health class? It's not regular for a while, Jazz. Jeez."

"Well, ex*cuse* me! I'll make sure to keep my locker well stocked from now on," Jazz sniped.

Lo crossed her arms. "Look, this is getting us nowhere. I'll go find something," she told her. "Just...wait here."

"What are you going to do?" Jazz asked.

"I don't know," Lo admitted. "Just stay in the stall. If a teacher comes in, pull your feet up so they can't see you."

"Okay. Just hurry up."

"Trust me. I want this to be over as much as you do," Lo said.

"I seriously doubt that," Jazz said sourly. "You sure you can handle this?"

Lo smiled in spite of herself and gave Jazz what she hoped was a very Doctor-like look.

"You know me," she said. "I'm an optimist. A hoper of crazy hopes and dreamer of impossible dreams."

Jazz grinned. "Well, okay then, Doctor."

Lo pulled the door open and then turned back to look at Jazz.

"Allons-y!"

FORTY-FIVE

The halls were still deserted. The bell had rung ages ago, and Lo was now officially super late for class, probably being marked absent at this very moment. She had checked every girls' bathroom. She had even snuck into the senior boys' bathroom, in case, for some weird reason, it had once been a girls' room. Nothing. That had been a long shot anyway. Also, it was absolutely disgusting in there. It smelled like pee and armpits. And despite there being no pads anywhere, there was a condom machine attached to the wall. Lo studied it, then reached out and jiggled the knob, watching in disbelief as a little foil-wrapped package popped out and landed in the tray.

They were free?

Lo shook her head and shrugged. She supposed she could try asking for pads in the office.

Lo shuddered.

No, she couldn't do it.

She couldn't imagine asking Mrs. Parker, who was at least eighty years old, if she had a pad.

God.

Lo would make Jazz stuff a wad of paper towels down her pants before she went and asked the school secretary for a pad.

Then she turned the corner and spotted Marika still at her locker.

Oh, thank God!

"Marika!"

Lo was so relieved to find someone she actually knew that she almost hugged her.

"Hey, Lo." Marika looked up. "Still trolling for quarters?"

"No. But…this is awkward…" Lo swallowed. Why was this so hard to talk about? They'd all get their periods eventually!

"Okay," Marika said patiently.

"Listen…do you have a pad? I mean…I don't know if you…have…or use them…whatever. I need to find a pad. For my friend."

"Oh." Marika nodded. "Yeah, sure."

She reached into the depths of her locker and pulled one out, palming it to Lo surreptitiously. Like she was handing her a top-secret document or something.

"Thank you! Oh my god. You're saving us here."

"Wait. Is that what you needed the quarter for?" Marika asked.

Lo nodded.

"All the machines are empty," Marika said.

"Yeah. I found that out after searching the entire school."

"Crazy, right?" Marika shook her head.

"It's so stupid," Lo complained. "What are you supposed to do if you get your period and you don't have stuff?"

Marika shrugged.

"Well, someone should do something about it," Lo said.

Marika studied her. "Yeah. Someone should," she said mildly.

FORTY-SIX

Jazz was still hiding out in a stall when Lo returned to the bathroom.

"What took you so long?" Jazz called through the door.

"Here." Lo handed the pad over the stall door along with the gym sweats she had grabbed from her locker.

"Thanks, Lo."

Lo could hear the relief in Jazz's voice.

"You wouldn't believe what I had to go through to get that," Lo told her.

"Where did you get it?" Jazz asked through the door. "The office?"

Lo cringed. "God no! Can you imagine? I ran into Marika and asked her."

"You didn't tell her it was for me, did you?"

"Funnily enough, your name didn't come up," Lo said dryly.

Jazz came out of the stall, tying the drawstring of Lo's sweats and holding her own, which she'd rolled up into a ball. She walked to the garbage can and threw them in.

"You could have washed them," Lo told her.

"Nah. I'd always think of them as my period pants." She smiled a bit.

"Ha. Yeah."

Jazz sighed. "Listen. What you did. I really appreciate it," she said, not meeting Lo's eyes.

Lo nodded. "I know things are weird, Jazz. But we've been through too much for me to totally desert you." She thought of the Doctor suddenly. Because impossible and amazing things might be happening in the girls' bathroom, of all places.

"Thanks," Jazz said simply. But that one word was enough to bridge at least a little bit of the gap between them.

FORTY-SEVEN

Jazz wanted to go home. She told Lo she had cramps and just wanted to lie down and eat chocolate ice cream and Chewy Chips Ahoy! and watch a romantic movie that would make her cry.

Getting her period sounded less and less like something Lo *ever* wanted to go through. She walked Jazz to the office, chatting about random things to pass the time and fill the silence as they trudged down the halls together. But she finally couldn't take it anymore. She had to ask.

"Jazz?"

"Yeah?"

"What does it feel like?"

"Getting your period?" Jazz paused, thinking for a minute. "I don't know. I get cramps. Not normal cramps. Weird ones that feel like my insides are all twisted up. Sometimes they're really bad and my back aches and nothing really makes it stop. When it's that bad, I usually feel kind of sick too. Like I'm going to throw up. Not really much else. Like, I can't usually feel the blood coming out or anything. Obviously. Or I would have noticed before you tackled me." Her cheeks went red as she remembered.

"And do you feel different?" Lo asked.

"What do you mean?"

"Do you feel older or anything?"

Jazz stopped walking, thinking before she answered. "I guess I did at first," she said. "It seemed like such a big deal the first time. But right now I feel exactly the same as I did before I got it. Except for one thing."

"What?"

"I really want a shower." She shuddered. Then she looked at Lo and they both started laughing. For a second it felt like old times.

FORTY-EIGHT

Lo had the kind of mom she could tell almost anything to. Even if it was a little awkward for her. Her mom had basically made it clear that nothing was off-limits, and no matter what was going on, Lo knew her mother would listen. And this time Lo needed someone to listen. Someone older and wiser than she was. Because if she was being honest, she still didn't feel any older than nearly thirteen.

She made them each a cup a tea and sat down on the couch beside her mom. Her dad was puttering around the kitchen, throwing something together for dinner, so they had a chance to talk alone. She tucked her feet under her, took a deep breath and poured out the story of her day and what had happened to Jazz.

"I mean, it makes no sense," Lo ranted. "I had to walk around the school until I found someone with a pad. There are literally no pads or tampons anywhere in the entire school. Every single machine is empty." Lo shook her head. "But they give out condoms in sex ed like they're Halloween candy or something! And they have a machine for *those* in the senior boys' bathroom! And!" Lo took a deep breath before getting to the absolute kicker. "AND *those* machines are free!"

"Yeah, that's definitely a double standard," her mom said.

"And do you know what the point is?" Lo asked. "The freakin' point is that all the girls at that school, at one time or another, will actually *need* pads! How many of the kids need condoms? But the school gave out handfuls of those free after sex ed! Why do they give out condoms and have machines full of them for free, but girls can't even *pay* to get pads! I know it's not the same, but it's not fair," she finished.

"You're right," Lo's mom agreed.

Lo stared at her. "Really? I mean, I am, right? I know I am." She paused. "I think I am."

"You are. It's sexist," her mom said.

Lo nodded emphatically. "Yes! It's sexist! That's exactly what it is. I just couldn't think of the right word!"

"So what are you going to do about it?" Lo's mom asked, setting her teacup down and studying her daughter.

Lo reared back. "Me?"

"Of course. Do you want to let it go, or do you want to do something about it?"

Lo realized she hadn't really considered it. "What can *I* do?" she asked. "I'm just a kid. No one is going to listen to me."

"Well, that's up to you," her mom said. "You have a voice, Lo. Do you want to use it? Whatever you decide, I'll help if you want me to."

Taking a sip of tea, Lo rolled the idea around. If no one else was going to do anything, maybe she could. Couldn't she? "Yeah! I mean, maybe I could start by talking to the principal." The thought of *that*, of sitting down across from Mr. Cohen and talking about periods, was enough to make her want to die. She'd literally rather do *anything* other than that. She'd rather let tarantulas crawl over her face. She'd rather eat goat eyeballs. She'd almost rather run outside naked than talk to Mr. Cohen about periods.

Almost.

But it wasn't fair. Boys were always treated differently than girls.

It was sexist.

And if no one else was going to do something about it, Lo decided she would step up and use her voice. She might be a kid, but she'd make Mr. Cohen listen.

"Will you come with me?" she asked her mom.

"I'd be proud to," her mom said, and she wrapped her arms around her and gave her a hug that made Lo feel like an equal. Like an actual grown-up.

Dear Doctor,

Why does it feel like girls are treated like…like aliens? I mean, why is it okay for the school to hand out free condoms but not have pads or tampons for the girls? Why are the normal bodily functions of girls treated like a deep, dark secret and something to be ashamed of, but they're handing out condoms like candy canes? Boys are treated so differently, and it's not fair. I got into trouble for giving Bobby Zucker a wedgie. And Mr. Cohen was right to punish me for it. But the boys were being disgusting. They were harassing the girls, and nothing happened to them. Honestly. Why would I want to grow up when that's what I can expect?

My mom says I should use my voice to speak out against inequality and sexism, but I've always just kind of let Jazz speak up for both of us.

But she's not speaking for me anymore, and I don't want her to. I think I want to see if someone will listen to what I have to say.

Maybe I really am growing up.

Your friend always,

Lo

FORTY-NINE

That night Lo sat in bed with her laptop and googled "how to avoid getting your period." It was a little weird, she knew that. But there was *no* way *in hell* she was going to risk having *her* period start during class for the whole school to see.

Most of the online articles said that the birth-control pill could control it. But she didn't even *have* her period yet. And she wasn't planning on having sex for a *really* long time. Maybe never. And there was no way her mom was going to put her twelve-year-old daughter on the pill.

She read that eating pineapple kept it away. She already *did* that. She loved pineapple. Maybe she was already keeping her period away and didn't even know it! Maybe that was why she seemed to be the last person on the entire planet who hadn't gotten it yet.

She read about eating gram lentils, but she didn't even know what gram lentils were.

She read about eating spicy food and figured she could probably do that. But then she read something that said she had to *stop* eating spicy food.

Or eat more green beans.

Or herbs.

Or watermelon.

Or chia seeds.

Lo slammed her laptop closed.

There was no way watermelon was going to do it.

Lo leaned back against her pillows, trying to turn her brain off so she could sleep, but it was still full of chia seeds and pineapple and periods.

She turned and punched her pillows into a better shape, then flopped back down on them with a long, dramatic sigh.

Lo turned over and caught sight of the jar with the chrysalis in it on her dresser. Her mom must have moved it back into her room. She got up and walked over to the jar, fully expecting to see the chrysalis all dried up and shriveled with the butterfly, black and dead, wrapped inside it.

But to her utter shock, the chrysalis wasn't black anymore!

Through the thin skin of the chrysalis, Lo could see the sleeping butterfly's orange-and-black wings wrapped snugly around it.

It was still alive in there!

If that butterfly could survive going through a change like this, then Lo figured she could probably handle whatever was going to happen to her too.

FIFTY

What did you wear to school when you planned to confront your notoriously mean, very intimidating school principal about the lack of period products available to students?

Lo had been staring into her closet for what felt like an hour, and it was getting late. She wanted to avoid anything pink. Pink didn't seem serious enough. And, truthfully, it reminded her too much of blood.

She pulled on a pair of jeans and a plain black T-shirt, but that didn't seem right. She didn't feel like herself. She pulled out a floaty-looking button-up shirt she had bought online but had never gotten around to wearing. She pulled it on and tied the front. It was a little dressy, but if you looked really closely, there were little Daleks all over it.

Perfect.

"Nice shirt," her dad said, sticking his head around the doorway. "Are you ready for your meeting?"

Lo still felt a little weird talking to her dad about this stuff. But she was trying really hard not to, so she took a deep breath and smiled. "Yeah. I think so."

"You're going to be great," he told her. "The Doctor would be proud."

"Thanks, Dad!" Lo ran over and hugged him tightly before heading down the stairs.

"Well? How do I look?" she asked her mom, twirling past the kitchen table cluttered with plates of pancakes, butter and syrup, orange juice and coffee.

"You look good. Are you nervous?" her mom asked.

Lo shook her head and said yes at the same time.

"Don't be," her mom said. "You're in the right. And I'll be right there beside you."

"It's just a weird subject to bring up with the principal," Lo admitted. Truthfully, it was a pretty awkward subject to bring up with *anyone*. But Lo was quickly realizing how wrong that was. If things were going to change, someone was going to have to talk about it.

"I know. But it shouldn't be," her mom told her, basically reading her mind. "Every woman gets their period. We should be able to talk about it without being embarrassed."

Lo nodded, then frowned. "But nobody does," she said. "Why is that? No one writes books about it or puts it in movies. We pretend it doesn't happen when we all know that it does. It's so dumb that we have to be embarrassed about it."

"Well, maybe you can change that," her mom said, kissing her on the top of her head.

Maybe she could. But right now, all Lo could think about was not throwing up on her shoes.

Dear Doctor,

I have no idea what I'm going to say! How do I talk to a man who has never said more than two words to me about periods and how sexist it is to turn a blind eye to what the girls in his own school need? I need some advice.

Wait. Maybe I can just do what you said in "The Doctor, the Widow and the Wardrobe." I'll just hang on and pretend it's part of the plan. You're the best.

Lo

FIFTY-ONE

Lo and her mother sat outside the principal's office on blue plastic chairs that were rock hard and had probably been there since the eighties. Lo didn't even want to attempt the math to figure out how many butts had been planted there before hers. Ick. She shifted, trying to get comfortable and willing her heart to slow down so she could figure out what she was going to say.

"Lauren?" the principal's secretary called out.

"Yeah? Sorry. I mean, yes?" Lo waved.

"He'll see you now."

Lo looked at her mom, panicking.

"What do I say?" she hissed desperately.

Her mom smiled gently.

"Just be yourself, Lo. Say exactly what you said to me. And I'll back you up."

"Promise?" Lo asked.

"Always."

Her mom would make an excellent Companion.

FIFTY-TWO

"So. What can I do for you, Miss…?" Every time Lo saw her principal, her first thought was that he looked exactly like what you'd expect for a middle-school principal: Balding. A mustard stain on his hideous tie. A frown clouding his already unpleasant face.

"Simpson," Lo finished for him.

"Right. Miss Simpson. What can I do for you? Or…your mother?" He reached out a hand to Lo's mom.

"This is Lauren's meeting," her mom said. "I'm just here for moral support."

He nodded. "All right then. Lauren?"

"Right." She cleared her throat. Glanced at her mom. Her hands were sweating, so she wiped them nervously on her pants and took a deep breath. "A friend of mine got her… umm, her period and didn't have…umm…a pad with her."

Lo swallowed hard and tried to shake the automatic feeling of embarrassment she always got when talking about anything even remotely personal. *Come on, Doctor. Help me out. Help me be brave!* She took a deep breath and tried again. "And all of the machines in the girls' bathrooms are empty." She sounded a lot stronger now.

The principal's face had turned red. Already. She had barely gotten started, and he was the color of a tomato. Clearly Lo wasn't the only one embarrassed by this.

"Oh. I see. Umm…I'm sorry to hear that." He cleared his throat. Then cleared his throat again. Awkwardly. Not meeting her eyes. Then he stood up. "Okay then. Is that all? You should probably get to your class now."

Lo looked at him incredulously.

He had just dismissed her!

And she was so sick and tired of people dismissing her! First Jazz and now Mr. Cohen.

Lo shook her head. No. She was *not* going to let anyone underestimate her ever again. Especially not a man with mustard on his tie.

"No! That is *not* all. Why doesn't the school have… supplies, anyway?" The principal sat back down. "What if we don't have anything and we get our period at school? What are we supposed to do then?" She stopped, breathing hard.

Her mom reached over and squeezed her hand.

"Well, Miss…umm…"

"Simpson!"

"Right. Miss Simpson. The school can't afford to provide… feminine products for free. We assume you girls are old enough to be responsible for keeping your own supplies on hand." He nodded, satisfied with his answer.

"Are you serious?" Lo exploded. It didn't matter that she was talking to the principal. This wasn't right. *He* wasn't right. "So girls are expected to be responsible for any supplies we might need, but you're okay with providing condoms for free? Apparently we're not expected to keep our lockers stocked with birth control. Just pads."

The principal gawked at her. "That…that's different," he stammered.

"How is it different?" Lo asked. She wasn't shaking anymore. She sounded grown-up. She sounded strong.

She sounded like the Doctor.

"We're being realistic and trying to prevent teen pregnancy." He sounded like he was reading from a book, and that made Lo even madder.

"You're not being realistic. You're being sexist!" Lo shot back. "It's not fair. Girls can't help getting their periods. The school pays for paper towels and tissues because they're necessary. So are pads and tampons, and we shouldn't be penalized for something we can't help. Something that happens to half the school population. Especially when the school can manage to pay for condoms." She looked over at her mom, who was smiling and nodding at her proudly. In that moment Lo had never loved her mother more. For being there and for letting her speak for herself and especially for not treating her like a little kid. She nodded back and stood up.

"Thanks for listening," Lo said. "But I think this is just the beginning of this conversation."

Dear Doctor,

I did it!

You should have seen me! You would have been so proud. I stood up to the principal and told him the school policies were sexist.

I can't believe I really did it. But I thought of you, and suddenly I wasn't scared anymore.

It felt like you were right there with me.

Your friend,

Lo

FIFTY-THREE

By lunchtime the halls were buzzing, absolutely *buzzing*, with the news that Lo Simpson had called a meeting with the principal. No one was sure what it was about, but everyone was speculating.

"I heard she told him off for not letting girls try out for football," one kid said.

"I heard she complained that we don't have vegan food in the caf," another student said.

"Well, *I* heard she told him that they should put condoms in the girls' bathrooms."

"Seriously?"

Yup. Buzzing. It was insane.

MJ waylaid Lo by her locker. "Did you really tell the principal to put condoms in the girls' bathrooms?"

"What? No! Who said that?"

"Everyone's talking about it," MJ told her.

"About what?" Lo asked.

"About *you*! And your meeting with Mr. Cohen."

"But how did everyone find out?" Lo squeaked. "Did you tell anyone?"

"Of course not. But it's middle school," MJ said wisely. "There are no secrets in middle school."

Jazz stepped between them from out of absolutely nowhere. "I heard you met with Mr. Cohen," she said.

Lo shrugged.

"So what was the meeting about? Condoms?" Jazz asked.

"Oh, for crying out loud, does everyone think that's what it was about?"

"Yes!" Jazz and MJ yelled in unison.

"I was just asking her the same thing," MJ said. She turned back to Lo. "So?"

"It was not about condoms! I told him it wasn't fair that girls have to pay for…" *Oh, come on, Lo. Just say it!* Lo looked around to see if anyone was listening, then whispered, "Pads and tampons."

"You said that to the principal?" Jazz gasped.

"Yes! I told him it wasn't fair when they're handing out condoms to the entire school for free."

"I never even thought of that," MJ mused.

Jazz snickered at MJ's expression.

"And…I called him sexist," Lo admitted.

"You did not!" Jazz shrieked.

"I did!" She giggled. "I told the principal that he was sexist."

"Oh my *god*!" MJ doubled over, laughing.

"You are such a badass," Jazz told her admiringly.

"Yeah, I am." Lo smiled. "I'm a total badass." For the first time in her life, Lo didn't feel like the sidekick. She felt like the hero.

FIFTY-FOUR

"So I've been thinking," Lo said to MJ as they sat in the cafeteria at lunch, "and I think we have to do something."

"What do you mean?" MJ asked. Zev was on their phone, scrolling Instagram and apparently oblivious to the conversation going on around them.

"It's not fair that the school thinks it's okay to provide condoms and toilet paper and paper towels for the students but not pads and tampons. I tried to talk to the principal, but he wouldn't listen to me. And if we want things to change, we need to do something about it ourselves."

"Do something about what?" Jason threw himself down beside MJ in his customary fashion and started digging enthusiastically through his lunch bag. He looked less American Eagle and more Hot Stuff today. The store, not, you know, as a commentary on his actual appearance.

"Nothing!" Lo shook her hair in front of her face. She

saw Jaden watching this exchange and smirking, and she avoided his eyes.

"Actually,"—Zev put their phone down—"isn't it just as sexist to exclude us from your conversation?"

Crap.

Zev turned to Jason. "They're talking about how it's sexist for the school to provide condoms but not pads and tampons. There." They picked up their phone again. "You're welcome."

"God, Zev!" MJ squealed.

To Lo's utter shock, Jason didn't look embarrassed at all.

"You do know I have two moms, right?" He unwrapped his sandwich and bit into it, chewing thoughtfully. "I know all about periods, and it's no big deal. And I think you're right. I never even thought about it, but that *is* sexist."

MJ nodded enthusiastically. "But what can *we* do?" she asked. "No one is going to listen to a bunch of kids."

Lo looked around the table. MJ's ears were a little pink, but Zev and Jason looked like talking about periods was completely normal. And Lo realized suddenly that this was the way it should be! She sat back and folded her arms.

"We could start a petition," Lo suggested. "If we can get enough girls to sign it, we could bring it back to the principal. He'd have to listen if enough of us complain."

"Yes!" MJ said. "That's brilliant, Lo!"

"It is," Zev agreed.

Lo grinned suddenly. "I can't believe that I thought of it! But, just like the Doctor, I'm being very clever here."

"Well, *I'm* impressed," MJ told her.

"Me too," Jason agreed, cocking his head to the side. "You're different, Lo. More…confident."

She was, Lo realized. She really was.

FIFTY-FIVE

"So where do we start?" MJ asked.

"Yeah, Lo," Jason said. "This is your idea. What do you think we should do?"

Zev nodded their head enthusiastically.

"We?" Lo asked. Did Zev and Jason really want to help? She wouldn't have thought in a million years that she'd be having this conversation with them, but here they were. And if this kind of thing could ever be completely normal and not at all humiliating, it had to start somewhere.

"Of course *we*," Zev told her. "We all want to help."

Lo looked at them, glancing between MJ, Zev and Jason, who were staring at her, waiting for her to tell them what to do. She'd never been the one in charge before. Never in her entire life.

"Ummm…" she began, and then cleared her throat. She thought about the Doctor and tried again. "Okay. Well, I could write up the petition." They were all nodding at her. She could do this, she thought. She could. "I'll print copies, and we can get all the other girls to sign them."

"We should get the boys to sign them too," Jason said. "Zev and I can handle that, if you want."

"Why would the boys want to sign?" MJ asked.

"Because stuff like this isn't just a girl issue. It's a human issue," he said.

Huh.

"What do we do with them once they're signed?" Zev asked.

"We take them to the principal," Lo told them. "If enough people sign them, he can't say no."

She looked at them for a second.

"There's one other thing," she said. "Do you have any money?"

FIFTY-SIX

"What do we buy?" Lo asked MJ, staring around the store at all the boxes of tampons and pads stacked floor to ceiling in aisle three. There seemed to be endless choices. Some had wings. Some didn't. Lo didn't know what the wings were for, but she figured wings had to be a good thing.

There was light absorbency. Ultra. Regular. Super. Super plus.

It was mind-boggling.

"Have you even had your period yet?" MJ asked.

Lo shook her head, shrugging. "No. Have you?"

"Yeah. For about five months now."

Lo sighed with relief. "That's why I need you. There are way too many choices. How do you know which to get?"

"I use these," MJ said, plucking a box of something called Teen Pads off the shelf.

"Okay. Well, let's get a bunch of boxes of those. And some tampons, I guess. Zev and Jason are grabbing baskets at the

Dollar Shop, so that's done. We can fill those and put some in each bathroom."

"Yes! With a note so everyone knows they can take what they need," MJ said.

"Right."

"Then let's get started," MJ said, grabbing an armful of tampon boxes and heading to the counter, not caring at all who saw her. Lo stared at her in admiration, then grabbed a few herself.

MJ nudged her shoulder against Lo while they waited in line. "This is a really great idea, Lo. I mean it."

Lo smiled. "We make a good team," she said.

MJ smiled back. "We sure do."

FIFTY-SEVEN

MJ, Zev and Jason were filling the baskets while Lo wrote little signs for them on index cards her dad had found, when her mom came home from work. Lo had texted her, so she wasn't shocked by the crowd or the mess.

"Hi, everyone," she said, kissing Lo on the head.

"Hi, Mom. These are my friends Jason and Zev, and you know MJ," she said, pointing them out as she said their names.

"Right. Nice to meet you all," her mom said, smiling. She took in all the clutter. "So what are you up to?"

"We pooled our money and bought supplies for the girls' bathrooms," she said.

"Really?" her mom asked, surprised. She had probably thought that Lo was building a papier-mâché model of the TARDIS or something. To be fair, it wouldn't have been the first time.

"We're also writing a petition to get the school to pay for pads and tampons," MJ said.

Her mom was quiet, watching as Lo wrote another sign that said:

Women's Rights = Equality for All! Take what you need.

"That's really amazing," her mom said quietly.

Lo glanced up and smiled. "Thanks Mom."

She honestly didn't care what anyone else thought. She just knew this was something she had to do. It was one thing to hear praise from her friends, but it was something completely different to hear it from her mother. Her mom's words made her feel all warm inside.

Her mom put an arm around her shoulder. "I'm really proud of you. All of you!"

"Me too!" her dad said as he wandered in with a bowl of chips for them.

Lo smiled at her friends. Zev was beaming, and Jason grinned at her.

"Thank you!" MJ said. "It was a team effort."

"I can see that," her mom said. "Well, let me know if we can help with anything, okay?"

"Well…could you maybe donate a couple of boxes of tampons?" Lo asked. It was getting easier to talk about, she noticed. Even with Jason and Zev and her dad there, she didn't feel embarrassed anymore.

Her mom smiled again. "Absolutely," she said, hugging Lo tightly.

FIFTY-EIGHT

We the undersigned respectfully ask that the school provide ~~feminine~~ products for free in the girls' bathrooms. The school provides toilet paper and paper towels for free because they're necessary for normal bodily functions. Periods are also a normal bodily function. We don't choose to get our periods. ~~Feminine~~ products are just as necessary to us as paper towels and toilet paper. We should not be penalized because we are girls. We ask that the school consider providing these necessary supplies for free.

FIFTY-NINE

"Wait." Zev frowned, putting the petition down. "We need to change this."

"Change what?" Lo asked.

"I don't think it should say 'feminine products,'" they said.

"Why not?" MJ asked, looking over their shoulder at the petition.

"It's not inclusive."

"What do you mean?" Jason asked.

"Well, it's not just girls who get their periods. What about trans boys? Or people who are nonbinary? We should word it so it doesn't exclude anyone, whether they're 'feminine' or not," they said, making air quotes with their fingers. "And we should make sure all the bathrooms have baskets."

"Good point." Lo nodded. "All right then. What should it say, Zev?"

SIXTY

We the undersigned respectfully ask that the school provide ~~feminine~~ menstrual products for free in all of the ~~girls'~~ bathrooms. The school provides toilet paper and paper towels for free because they're necessary for normal bodily functions. Periods are also a normal bodily function. We don't choose to get our periods. ~~Feminine~~ Menstrual products are just as necessary to us as paper towels and toilet paper. ~~We should not be penalized because we are girls.~~ We should not be punished for getting our periods. We ask that the school consider providing these necessary supplies for free in every school bathroom.

SIXTY-ONE

"There." Lo sat back and looked at their new petition.

"Perfect," Zev said and smiled.

"I like that," MJ agreed. "Now we're including everyone."

"Okay. So now that it's perfect, what do we do with it?" Jason asked.

Lo scratched her ear thoughtfully. "Well, we bring copies to school—with a bunch of blank pages—and we get girls to sign it," she said.

"And boys," Jason interjected.

"And trans and nonbinary kids," Zev added.

"Boys and girls and variations thereupon," MJ half-quoted.

"Right! Sorry. We let anyone who wants to sign it, sign. No exclusions."

"Yeah!" MJ cheered.

"We meet up at lunch and we get signatures," Lo said.

"What if no one signs it?" MJ asked.

Lo thought about that for a second and then grinned.

"We don't give up. We're taking a stand. Like the Doctor in 'The Pandorica Opens.' Remember when he stood up and reminded all the aliens who he was and they shouldn't mess with him? Well, that's what we're doing. We're standing up for what's right. No matter what," she said.

"Yes!" Jason high-fived her.

"Then it's a plan," Zev said.

"Allons-y!" MJ yelled, throwing her fist in the air.

Damn, thought Lo. *That was my line.*

SIXTY-TWO

Between the four of them, MJ, Jason, Zev and Lo had gotten signatures from 183 kids.

They really did make quite a team.

They settled down around their table in the caf at lunch and tried to work out the rest of their plan.

"It's not enough. I really wanted to hit two hundred," Lo said.

"Well, who haven't we asked?" MJ looked around the cafeteria.

"We've asked pretty much everyone in seventh and eighth grade." Zev frowned.

"You could ask the sixth graders," a voice said from behind Lo. Jazz and Abbi had wandered over from the It Girls' table.

"I got my period in sixth grade," Abbi said.

"Jason and Zev showed us your petition. We signed it," Jazz said hurriedly. "Ummm…"

Wow, Lo thought. Jazz was never at a loss for words.

"And?" Lo asked.

"And…what you're doing is really cool." Jazz blushed.

"It was Lo's idea," Zev said.

"Really?" Abbi asked, frowning.

"Hard to believe, right?" Lo smirked.

"No!" Jazz nudged Abbi with her shoulder. "No, it's not. Look, it's really cool. And we want to help," she said.

"Both of us," Abbi added, looking contrite. "I always thought it was so dumb the school doesn't have pads in the bathrooms. But I didn't know we could actually do anything about it. It's, like, really cool. What you're doing, I mean."

Well, holy cow. Abbi was actually being…human!

"So can we help?" Jazz asked.

"Yeah, sure. If it's okay with everyone else?" Lo looked around the table.

"Fine with me." MJ shrugged.

"Me too," Jason said. "Zev?"

"Sure."

"Okay then," Lo said. "Let's ask the sixth graders." She handed a page to Jazz. "Wait. What about the teachers?"

"What about them?" Abbi asked.

"I bet some of them would sign it. Especially if they have to remember to bring their own tampons and pads from home too."

"Okay," MJ said. "I'll come with you to find teachers, and everyone else can talk to the sixth graders and any other seniors who aren't in the caf."

"Good luck asking Ms. Falkenstein to sign it," Zev said with a snicker.

Lo shuddered. Frankenstein would probably grab the petition and rip it to shreds.

SIXTY-THREE

Approaching a teacher to talk about *anything* having to do with puberty was awkward at best. Even with Lo's new comfort level with the subject. They were *teachers, for crying out loud!*

But Lo was determined to get as many people's signatures as humanly possible before handing the petition over to Mr. Cohen.

The first few times she'd walked up to a teacher, she'd just handed the clipboard to them and waited for them to read it themselves. So far all but one had signed. But by the time she and MJ were halfway through the teachers, she was explaining the whole thing to them.

"We already brought in baskets of menstrual products for all the bathrooms," she told Miss McEwan, the resource teacher. "But we think the school should have to pay for it."

"I agree," she told them, reaching for the pen MJ was holding.

"Thanks! I wasn't sure the teachers would sign, but like the Doctor says, it's a sign of weakness to be certain of anything."

"Which doctor, dear?" Miss McEwan asked, handing the clipboard back.

MJ snickered, then pretended to cough to cover it up.

"What's this?" an icy voice asked over Lo's shoulder. *Oh crap. Ms. Falkenstein.*

"Umm...nothing?" Lo said, shoving the clipboard behind her.

"Don't blink," MJ whispered.

Right. *If you blink, you're dead.* Just like the Doctor and the Weeping Angels, who only attacked when you weren't looking at them, you never wanted to take your eyes off Frankenstein, just in case she pounced.

"May I see that, Lauren?" Ms. Falkenstein said in a voice that demanded rather than asked.

Lo sighed and handed it over. Falkenstein was sure to take it and throw it away.

Or shred it.

Or give them detention until the end of time. Lo looked at MJ. If Frankenstein tried, she'd grab the clipboard and run. She really would.

The teacher read it silently, then looked at Lo, then MJ.

Studying them like slides under a microscope.

"May I borrow your pen?" she asked suddenly.

MJ held it out wordlessly.

Lo was sure she was going to draw a big X through it or something. She mentally prepared herself to snatch the clipboard back, even if she ended up being expelled. It would be worth it. She was not about to let Frankenstein destroy their hard work. It was too important.

But as she watched, Ms. Falkenstein added her neat signature to the bottom of the page before handing it back.

"Good for you, girls," she said, offering them a slight smile and nod before turning and walking back toward her class.

Lo and MJ stared at each other without saying a word before running off to find the rest of the group.

SIXTY-FOUR

"You are not going to *believe* who just signed the petition!" MJ yelled, waving the clipboard in front of Jazz and Abbi when they all met back up in the caf. "Falkenstein!" she shrieked before either of them could venture a guess.

"You lie!" Zev said, grabbing the clipboard and reading it. "Oh my god. You're not lying. She really signed it."

"And she told us 'good job,'" Lo said.

"And *smiled*!" MJ finished. "I didn't even know her face could do that!"

Lo still couldn't believe it had happened. "How many did you get?" she asked.

"More than we needed," Jason said, grinning. "With the teachers and the sixth graders, us and our parents…" He did a quick count. "Two hundred and thirty-six."

Lo and MJ screamed and jumped up and down, hugging each other. Then Lo pulled Jason and Zev into a group hug. Abbi and Jazz watched awkwardly until Lo yanked them into the circle too. Lo had never thought in a million years she'd ever hug Abbi, but if there was one thing they could ever hug about, it was this. It felt like they had won a battle. They all just wanted to be treated the same as everyone else.

"Ready to take this to Mr. Cohen?" Jason asked her.

"Yeah." Lo nodded. "You know why? Because the War Doctor says we don't ever give in, and he's right!"

"We've got the Pandorica, so we've got the world," Jason yelled.

"What's a Pandorica?" Abbi asked.

Dear Doctor,

We did it! We actually did it! We got the signatures.
Now it's time to stand up to the villain—Mr. Cohen—
and demand equality.

Because we deserve it. It's our right.

And if Mr. Cohen won't listen, we'll just have to make
him listen. I'm not going to let anyone silence me ever
again.

Your friend,

Your Companion,

Lo

SIXTY-FIVE

The group marched—literally marched—to the principal's office.

They marched side by side, all six of them in a row, arms linking them together.

"We'd like to see Mr. Cohen, please," Lo announced to the school secretary.

"I heard you'd be coming after lunch," Mrs. Parker whispered, winking broadly at them. "Everyone's talking about your petition." She looked around furtively. "Can I sign it?" she asked.

Abbi held their clipboard out for a final signature. The secretary signed it with a flourish, then picked up her phone and buzzed the principal.

"I have six kids here to see you, sir," she said. "Yes, it's important." She winked at them again and smiled. "Go right in," she told them. "Good luck."

"Thanks," Lo said. She looked at MJ, Jason, Zev, Jazz and Abbi. "Whatever happens in there, I want you to know I couldn't have done this without all of you."

"Yes, you could have," Jazz told her. "You've changed, Lo. You're like the Doctor. You're a madwoman with a box." She smiled.

Lo smiled back, but deep down she thought she had always felt this way. It was just that no one else had ever noticed before.

"I'm still scared though," Lo admitted.

MJ squeezed her hand. "It's okay to be scared. But like the Doctor says, the courageous thing is doing it anyway."

"Okay. Let's do this. 'If we're going down, we're going down in style…'"

"Like a Peruvian folk band!" Jason said. Five of them cracked up while the sixth looked absolutely perplexed by the conversation.

"What are you guys even talking about? Seriously. I don't understand half of what you're saying." Abbi shook her head.

"Don't worry. We'll introduce you to the Doctor when this is over." Lo laughed. "Well. Here we go." She took a deep breath. If there was ever a moment for it, this was it. "Allons-y!" She smiled.

Lo gathered all the pages of the petition onto one clipboard and led the way into Mr. Cohen's office.

SIXTY-SIX

"What can I do for you?" Mr. Cohen asked, tapping at his keyboard and basically ignoring them.

"Well, if we could have your attention for just a few minutes," Lo said, rather more sarcastically than she had intended.

The others gawked at her. Lo couldn't help but grin a little. She definitely wasn't the same person who had once followed Jazz wordlessly everywhere she went. She had really burst out of her cocoon.

So to speak.

Her words had the desired effect.

Mr. Cohen stopped typing and looked at her, then did a double take.

"Miss Simpson," he said, nodding. "We meet again. What can I do for you?"

He had been a real jerk the last time they spoke, and Lo knew better than to expect an apology or anything close to it. But there was no reason they couldn't move forward. She nodded back, taking a deep breath and willing her hands to stop shaking.

"Sir, we are only a small percentage of the population of the school, but we speak for all of us. It is completely unfair that the school pays for necessary hygiene items like toilet paper and paper towels. They even pay for condoms. But they won't pay for pads or tampons? We don't choose to get our periods, Mr. Cohen. We shouldn't be penalized for it. You provide supplies for basic bodily functions. Periods are also a basic bodily function. And the necessary hygiene products should be provided to us free of charge."

She handed him the pages of their petition.

"We have two hundred and thirty-six signatures," she said.

"Two hundred and thirty-seven," Jazz interjected.

"Right." Lo nodded. "Two hundred and thirty-seven. Students *and* staff. I have no doubt we could have gotten more if we'd spent more time. We donated our own money to put free supplies in all of the bathrooms, but with all due respect, sir, we shouldn't have had to. It's not our responsibility. It's yours. All we ask is that you take this and get whoever you need approval from to look at it. Can you promise us that, sir?"

Everyone stared Mr. Cohen down, daring him to argue. Daring him to decline.

He surprised them.

"I'm impressed," he said, leafing through the pages of their petition. "I can't promise the board will agree, but I *can* promise to bring this before them."

The group cheered. MJ and Lo high-fived.

"Believe it or not, I agree with you," he went on. "There shouldn't be a double standard and inequality in our school. But there are rules to how this works, unfortunately."

Lo stood up and extended her hand across the wide desk of the principal. "Thank you, sir. But with all due respect, if you're a good man, you don't need rules." She'd loved it when Matt Smith's Doctor had said that.

She shook his hand and ushered her friends out before he could say another word. They made it to the hallway before jumping up and down, screaming and hugging each other for the second time that day.

"We did it!" MJ screamed.

"No. Lo did it," Jazz said, smiling.

There was something in that smile. Some flicker. Some promise of a new friendship. A different and better friendship. Of starting over on equal ground.

"We *all* did it," Lo said.

"You were amazing in there," Zev told her.

"You really were," Jason agreed.

"I can't believe you just talked about periods with Mr. Cohen, Lo!" Abbi shrieked.

They laughed then. All six of them.

Together.

Dear Doctor,

I feel different.

For the longest time, I didn't want to grow up.

But if this is what growing up is about, then maybe I'm ready after all.

Because I made people listen to me. And I was brave when it mattered.

It's like you always say—the universe is a big place where impossible things happen, which we call miracles. And you know what? Today, with MJ and Jason and Zev and Jazz and Abbi? It felt like a miracle.

Thank you. Because I don't think I could have done any of this without the Doctor.

Your friend,

Lo

SIXTY-SEVEN

"Hey, Lo? Can I talk to you for a second?" Jason pulled her aside as the rest of the group continued down the hall, too busy reliving their victory and trying to explain *Doctor Who* to Abbi to notice them.

"Yeah, sure. What's up?"

"Ummm…so I was wondering if you wanted to hang out sometime? Like, maybe go to a movie or something?" The tips of his ears were bright pink.

"Oh! Oh wow." Lo felt herself blushing too. "Ummm… actually…the thing is, I don't think I'm ready to date yet," she said.

Jason nodded slowly. "Oh. Yeah, okay." He didn't seem upset at all. Lo was relieved about that. "So can we be friends though?" he asked with a smile.

"We're already friends!" The words surprised her, but it was true.

"We are, right? Cool! That's cool."

Lo grinned at him. It *was* cool. Really cool.

SIXTY-EIGHT

"Mom!" Lo ran into the house, taking the steps two at a time. "Mom! You're not going to believe what happened today!"

She dropped her bag on the floor and headed into the kitchen. Her mom wasn't home yet.

"Well, now who am I supposed to tell?" she grumbled to herself. Her dad wouldn't be home until after supper.

Lo grabbed a granola bar and headed to her room. She threw herself down on her bed, ready to dive into a book. Or maybe watch *Doctor Who* on her laptop. One of her favorite episodes. Like "The Big Bang." She loved the Pandorica episode. The Doctor saving the entire universe was just about as cool as it got.

Just then Lo caught a glimpse from the corner of her eye of something moving.

A flutter.

She stood and walked across the room to her dresser, where a monarch butterfly was opening and closing her wings gently in the glass jar that had housed its chrysalis for weeks. She wanted to show her mom, show everyone, but she couldn't leave it in the jar where it might damage its papery orange-and-black wings.

Carefully, gently, she carried the jar into the backyard to the patch of garden where her mother had planted pink and yellow zinnias. Monarchs loved zinnias.

Lo unscrewed the lid of the jar and watched as the butterfly fluttered her wings in the sudden rush of air.

"Go on," Lo said. "Time for you to go."

The butterfly took tiny, delicate steps to the edge of the jar, spread her wings and soared.

Dear Doctor,

It's been a big year for me. I learned so many things about myself.

I learned that it's okay to speak up for yourself. And it's even better to speak up for people who may be afraid to speak up for themselves.

I learned that a good Companion is hard to find. And sometimes you find a bunch all at once.

I learned that friendship—real friendship—goes both ways.

I learned that I'm a lot braver than I ever thought I could be.

I learned that my mom will always have my back.

And I learned that I have people in my life who I can talk to. And maybe I don't need to write these letters anymore. I'll always need the Doctor in my life, but I don't feel alone anymore.

So thank you. Without you, I wouldn't be me.

Your friend always,

Lo

ACKNOWLEDGMENTS

When I started writing *Lo Simpson Starts a Revolution*, I wanted to write something about how brave and exciting the Doctor was, but it turned into a book about how brave and exciting kids can be. This came from my story and my daughter's story. It came from the firm belief that we need to stop being embarrassed about our bodies and the amazing things they do. Talking about periods and bras and gender identity and even sexuality is NOT wrong! And it's important. So is speaking out and standing up for each other.

So I'd like to thank those people who believed in this book and who continue to believe in me. My incredible agent, Amy Tompkins: I tell you this a lot, but I don't know what I'd do without you. The entire team at Orca, but especially my amazing editor Sarah Howden, who just instinctively understood me. Here's to many more adventures together. To my writing buddies, my dear friends, my cookies-and-milk crew: Paul Coccia, Heather Smith and Natasha Deen. You read this book before it was a book and you believed in it and in me and I can never thank you enough for that... especially Paul for those late-night texts. You know what I'm talking about. And to my family who has never doubted me for a minute. Chris, Josh and Taylor, I can never quite find the words to express how important you are to me and how much I love each of you. I think you know.

Melanie Florence is a writer of Cree and Scottish heritage based in Toronto. She was close to her grandfather as a child, and that relationship sparked her interest in writing about Indigenous themes and characters. She is the author of *Missing Nimâmâ*, which won the 2016 TD Canadian Children's Literature Award, *Stolen Words*, which won the 2018 Ruth and Sylvia Schwartz Children's Book Award, and the bestselling Orca Soundings titles *He Who Dreams* and *Dreaming in Color*.